Twelve Days of (Faerie) Christmas

CJ Brightley?

Also by C.J. Brightley

Erdemen Honor:
The King's Sword
A Cold Wind
Honor's Heir

A Long-Forgotten Song:
Things Unseen
The Dragon's Tongue
The Beginning of Wisdom

Fairy King
A Fairy King
A Fairy Promise

Other Works:
The Lord of Dreams

Twelve Days of (Faerie) Christmas

C.J. BRIGHTLEY

This book is a work of fiction. The characters, incidents, and dialogue are drawn from the author's imagination and are not to be construed as real. Any resemblance to actual events or persons, living or dead, is entirely coincidental.

ISBN: 9781985675537

Published in the United Sates of America by Spring Song Press, LLC.

www.cjbrightley.com

For my parents

ON DECEMBER 23

Charlotte's car ran out of gas on the way home from work. She sat, tears welling in her eyes, for several long minutes. The headlights of the cars behind her glared in the rearview mirror, and the tail lights gleamed bright red as they sped past her.

It really was too much.

Jim, her boss, had been in a truly, spectacularly bad mood for weeks, but today was the worst she'd ever seen. He'd snapped at Heather for making the coffee too weak, growled at the delivery man for putting the boxes in the wrong place, and grumped at Charlotte most of all. Her voice was too soft on the phone. She didn't print the papers for his meeting quickly enough, and the staple wasn't perfectly aligned with the top edge. Charlotte was of the opinion that a staple neatly angled at forty-five degrees was least likely to tear the paper, but her opinion was irrelevant. He didn't like her skirt (the houndstooth pattern was "garish"), he didn't like her handwriting on the messages she took while he was at the meeting ("too loopy"), and she hadn't realized the coffee pot was empty and made more so that it was ready when he wanted it (the pot was in the kitchen, so she couldn't see it from her desk).

And it was almost Christmas Eve! Charlotte had made cookies for everyone, and Heather had brought hot chocolate. She didn't think Jim had eaten any. He'd definitely skipped lunch, and probably breakfast too. Maybe he would have been in a better mood if he'd tasted her chocolate chip cookies and peppermint brittle. The stress of preparing for the big trial was wearing him down; Charlotte privately doubted he'd slept more than four hours a night since the beginning of November. The day had been utterly devoid of Christmas cheer and goodwill.

Running out of gas was the last straw.

She leaned forward to let her forehead rest against the steering wheel. "Please let tomorrow be better."

The nearest gas station was four miles ahead. This stretch of road had no sidewalks and no streetlights, although the lights from the shopping center shone cheerily. In the spring, the walk would be pleasant, but now, in the snow and sleet and in heels, the thought was daunting. She sighed and got out, hurrying to the shoulder before a passing car could hit her.

She didn't have a flashlight. Her phone would work, if the battery lasted long enough.

Her cute little kitten heels were entirely unsuited for walking through several inches of frozen slush. Her knee-length skirt was no protection against the wind and icy splashes from the passing traffic, and the shoulder of the road was uneven, pocked with broken bits of asphalt hidden under the snow.

She shivered and pulled her hood tighter around her head, frowning at the light of her phone as it played over the snow before her.

What a day.

The beam from her phone was only a faint glow that did little to light her path, but the headlights of passing cars helped.

The traffic grew more sporadic, and she made her way mostly by the light of the moon.

"What are you doing?" The voice on her right startled her so badly that her foot slipped out from under her, sending her flailing. With a surprised exclamation, the stranger grabbed her arms and steadied her.

"Who are you? Don't creep up on people in the dark!" Her words tumbled over each other. She backed away a little, her eyes straining to see him. Why couldn't there be cars now? She wanted their headlights full on him, perhaps someone to see if she waved for help. "I'm almost to the gas station. I already called someone. They're expecting me." It was a lie, and she didn't even feel guilty about it.

There was a moment of silence, and she stifled the urge to back away farther. Her heel was at the edge of a rather steep embankment, and it probably wouldn't improve matters if she went tumbling backwards down the slope.

"May I walk you there?" he said at last. "There is a little unpleasantness up ahead. I'd rather not have you pass unprotected."

She blinked. "Unpleasantness?" she asked.

He shook his head dismissively, which she could see only by the faint moonlight glinting off his hair. It was dark and perhaps wavy; it was hard to tell in the shadows. "Not a matter of much concern, but it will be safer if you are not alone. I will make myself a pleasant companion. Would you prefer conversation or silence?"

Charlotte shivered. "Um…" Her feet were so cold it was difficult to think. "I… whatever. Thanks."

"Are you cold?"

"Very." She pressed her lips together. She didn't want to cry.

"Would you like my coat? It's quite warm."

"No, I'm all right."

It was another lie. Her coat was *not* warm. She'd bought it to wear over her office clothes, intending to wear it between her car and the office or her townhouse. It was meant to look polished and add a thin layer during short walks, not keep a girl warm while walking miles in the snow.

He offered her his arm, a gallant gesture that made him seem less threatening. He walked between her and the road, though no more cars came.

His coat was thick and slightly fuzzy; she imagined it was made of exceptionally fine wool felt. Her fingers curled into the curve of his elbow.

After several minutes of silence, he said quietly, "You're shivering quite badly. Will you not accept my coat?"

It was true. Her feet were wet and cold, icy water had soaked her hose, the snow that had fallen on her head earlier had melted to dampen her hair…. Her voice shook when she said, "If you're sure you don't mind."

"Not at all." He slipped the heavy coat off and held it for her to slide her arms through the sleeves.

It was blissfully warm from his body heat, and she sucked in a relieved breath. "Thank you," she murmured, her teeth chattering. "Are you sure it's all right?"

"I'll be fine." He sounded both amused and pleased at her concern, and she glanced at him. She still had no idea what he looked like, but his voice was... intriguing. Deep but smooth, with a hint of an accent she imagined might be English or Irish, so faint it was difficult to identify. Not that she was particularly good at identifying accents. He offered his arm again, and this time when she slipped her fingers into the crook of his elbow, she felt the thin, soft material of his shirt over a lean, muscular arm.

Oh dear. The day had gotten both better and more terrifying.

"So! What are you doing walking around in the snow?" she said brightly.

She hadn't expected the question to make him hesitate, but he did. She glanced up at him, and he murmured, "Dealing with the unpleasantness I mentioned earlier. Pray don't ask me to elaborate. It's not fit for such lovely ears as yours."

Charlotte snorted softly with laughter. "Do you always flatter girls you've barely met and can barely see in the darkness?"

"I can see quite well. I forget you hu—" he stopped. "I forget not everyone can see in the dark."

She pondered that in silence for a moment. *I forget you humans...* was that what he'd almost said?

"What color is my nail polish?" she asked.

He glanced down, and chuckled, the sound like moonlight caressing her cheek. "You're not wearing any nail polish."

Then he stopped, putting his other hand over hers to draw her to a halt. She had the impression he was listening, but it was far too dark to see his expression.

Where were all the cars?

"Let me take you back to your car instead," he said quietly, and turned her around, one hand against her shoulder. The motion was graceful and entirely polite, but Charlotte stiffened.

"My car is out of gas. There's no point in going back without any gas." She tried to shrug away, but he drew her back the way they had come.

"I apologize, but I must insist." He glanced back over his shoulder, then down at her, the motion all but unnoticeable in the dark. "I'm quite sure I can induce your car to make it to a gas station."

"How can you do that?" Her voice rose in frustration. "It's out. It was running on fumes and it ran out of fumes. And I'm *hoping* it was just that I ran out of gas, because I really can't afford a new transmission or engine or whatever. And it was an awful day and I am *really* cold and..." Her eyes filled with tears. "And I really don't want to cry about how cold my feet are, but it's been that kind of day, and if you're not going to help, I'd appreciate it if you'd just leave me alone."

His voice softened, but he continued hurrying her in the same direction toward her car. "Ah, here we are. Get in and let me see what I can do."

The walk back to her car seemed remarkably short, given how long she'd been walking before she met him and then how far they had continued in the same direction after she'd met him. Charlotte scowled at the thought; perhaps his presence was more disconcerting than she'd realized at first. She almost pulled the car door closed with unnecessary force, then thought better of it, unwilling to risk smashing his fingers in the darkness.

"Try it now." His voice came through the window, slightly muffled by the glass and the wind. He hadn't done anything to the car, and she let out an irritated huff of breath. It was *out of gas*. How hard could that be to understand?

She turned the key, expecting the quiet click click of the engine doing exactly nothing.

It started without a protest, immediately pouring warm air onto her icy feet.

Charlotte gave a groan of relief and closed her eyes.

She rolled down the window to ask him if he needed a ride, but there was no one beside her door.

The headlights flooded the road ahead of her with light, and she flicked on her brights for a moment. A flash of white in the trees off to the right caught her eye, but then it was gone.

She was alone.

Charlotte drove to the nearest gas station. Only when she got out of the car and the frigid wind hit her did she realize that her car should not have warmed up so quickly. The man's heavy coat was still around her, and she pulled it tighter, feeling the soft texture of it. Perhaps it was the finest cashmere; the thick felt didn't have the scratchiness she'd always associated with wool. It smelled very faintly of woodsmoke and cedar. As she waited for the gas tank to fill, she noticed another masculine scent, like cologne or aftershave, so faint she hadn't noticed it at first, which gave her a reassuring impression of strength and comfort.

car remained warm and comfortable on the short drive home. She stepped through her front door with another sigh of relief, dropped her purse on the hall table, and kicked off her still-damp shoes. She pulled the coat off and hung it carefully in the coat closet. "I wish I knew how to get your coat back to you," she muttered. It looked expensive, and as disconcerted as she'd been by the man's abrupt disappearance, he'd been nothing but polite and helpful. She frowned, then stuck her hands in each pocket, wondering if one might contain a business card or some other piece of identification.

Success! She felt paper and pulled out a small, square envelope. The front was embossed with an intricate seal in gold foil on crisp white paper. The flap was not sealed, so she opened it.

December 24
10:30 PM
Old Town Alexandria Harbor

Charlotte frowned. There was no other information on the card. Of course the invitation wasn't for her, but perhaps she could find him at the harbor and return his coat. It felt like the least she could do after he'd gotten her car working again... however he'd managed it.

She sighed and put the envelope on the table beside her purse. She microwaved leftovers, ate hurriedly, and then took a hot shower. The water washed away the lingering chill in her toes and fingertips. Tomorrow was Friday, not to mention Christmas Eve, and she'd just stay in Old Town after work. She'd splurge and get a fancy appetizer for dinner at one of the expensive restaurants, bundle up, and watch the sun go down. The water was to the east, so it wouldn't exactly be sunset over the water, but she could sit on a bench near the water and watch the sun set over the trees and office buildings. She'd meet the mystery man and return his coat. How hard could it be?

ON CHRISTMAS EVE

Jim spent almost all of Christmas Eve in his office, emerging every three hours for more coffee and to snap at Charlotte and Heather when they were unfortunate enough to cross his path. Despite his irritability, he had Charlotte call in an order to the trendy bistro down the street for a sandwich delivery, complete with fancy little cupcakes, for all three of them. He paid; it felt like an apology for his mood, although he didn't say anything when he came to get his food and disappeared again immediately.

He was still in his office with his door closed as five o-clock came and went. Charlotte and Heather strolled out together.

"What are you doing tonight?" Heather asked.

"Meeting someone."

"Oh really?" Heather's eyebrows rose. "I thought you were still anti-men, after the whole He-who-shall-not-be-named fiasco."

Charlotte rolled her eyes tolerantly. "It's not a date. My car had an issue yesterday and he got it started again. He forgot his coat. I need to get it back to him."

"Name? Age? Marital status? Profession?"

"Don't know, don't know, don't know, and don't know." Charlotte frowned. "Sounds a bit creepy when I say it that way, doesn't it?"

"A bit, yeah. I'll stay with you."

Charlotte shook her head. "No, it's fine. I'll be right downtown."

"It's already dark. Don't be ridiculous."

"I'm getting spinach dip at Penrick's and then I'm huddling in a coffee house. I'm not going to get jumped."

Charlotte could tell her friend was unsure.

"I'll be fine, Heather. Really. If he was going to abduct me or something, he would have done it last night. No one else will have a chance because I'll be inside."

"Text me when you get home."

"I will."

"If I don't hear from you, I'm calling the police."

Charlotte smiled. "Thanks."

Heather's family had postponed the Christmas festivities for her, so she was on her way to the airport that night. She'd be arriving around the time Charlotte hoped to meet the mystery man at the harbor.

Penrick's was open until 8:00, so Charlotte lingered over her warm spinach dip and watched the snow begin to fall out the window.

"We're closing in ten minutes," the waitress said apologetically.

"Sorry. I'm done." Charlotte paid, calculating a generous tip and then adding ten dollars. "Merry Christmas."

"Wow. Thanks! You too!" The girl's eyes sparkled.

Charlotte wandered down the street. The coffee shop was open but nearly deserted; a bored young man slouched behind the counter. "What can I get you?"

"Hot chocolate, please." Waiting around was getting expensive, but she didn't want to sit there for hours without buying anything. She played with her phone for a while, then put it aside to focus on the book she'd brought.

"We close at ten." The voice brought her back to reality, and she looked around, disoriented for a moment. The coffee shop was still deserted. The bored young barista smirked slightly. "Good book?" he asked.

"Yeah, it is." She showed him the cover. "Merry Christmas." She walked out, and he locked the door behind her.

An icy blast hit her as she turned the corner, and she scowled at the gust. She made her way back to her car and retrieved the coat, then walked to the harbor, where the wind had whipped the tiny wavelets into froth. She found a bench and sat for a few minutes, but the metal seat was uncomfortably cold even through her jeans. So she stood and huddled in the lee of a building, wondering if, and when, the mystery man would appear.

A few minutes later, a dark figure strode briskly toward the pier.

Was it him?

She hesitated, but something about the set of his shoulders seemed familiar, even though she couldn't see his face and wouldn't have recognized it even in the light.

"Hello!" she called.

His head snapped toward her.

"It's me. From yesterday?" she said. "You left your coat. I brought it for you."

He looked away, focused on something over the water, and jogged to the edge of the pier. He knelt and seemed to watch the water; no, he was... reaching down? He grabbed something dark from beneath the pier, made a sudden jerking motion, and then seemed to fold it up until it disappeared.

Charlotte hung back, a little nervous both at the darkness and the man's strange actions.

The mystery man stood. "I take it you made it home safely."

"Yes, thanks." She held the coat out toward him.

"Thank you. I didn't expect to get it back." He pulled the heavy coat on over his button-down shirt. "It was kind of you to bring it." There was a questioning tone in his voice.

She shivered at a gust of wind. "No problem. I found a note in your pocket and hoped you'd be here."

The moonlight was brighter than it had been the previous night, and Charlotte saw the flash of the man's teeth as he smiled at her.

"I'm Charlotte," she said. "Thanks for last night. I made it to the gas station just fine."

"Good," he said.

She hesitated, then said, "I guess I should be going."

Something dark slithered from the water, wrapped around the man's leg, and jerked him off his feet. His elbow and head hit the heavy wood planks with sickening cracks. A second later he was yanked off the pier and into the water.

Charlotte shouted, but no sound answered her at first. The man had disappeared under the water with barely a splash.

There was a disturbance under the water, which Charlotte perceived only as a slight ripple in the darkness and an almost inaudible sound.

She pulled her phone from her pocket with trembling fingers and dialed.

"911. What's your emergency?"

"I'm at the harbor and someone just fell in." Her voice was shaking. "Maybe he can't swim. I can't see him anywhere."

"I've dispatched a team. How long ago did he fall in?"

"Just a minute ago."

The dispatcher asked several more questions while Charlotte stood uneasily on the pier. *Please, God, let him be all right.*

Without warning, the man pulled himself from the water, which cascaded from his coat in sheets, and sprawled face-down on the pier.

"He's out! He just came out."

"Is he breathing?"

"Sort of."

The man coughed and gagged, spilling more water across the boards to drip to the water below.

Charlotte hurriedly pushed the speaker button and set the phone down, then grabbed at the man's shoulders, intending to help him turn over.

He twisted to pin her arms behind her with one hand while the other held a blade to her throat.

Light caught the edge of his cheek, leaving his expression in shadow. The knife point produced a faint sting of pain at the edge of her jaw.

Charlotte sucked in a terrified breath, and for an instant, there was no sound but her heartbeat in her ears.

"Sorry," he rasped.

The knife disappeared, and he pulled away, only to double over again, coughing up more water.

The dispatcher's voice squawked. Charlotte picked up the phone with shaking hands. "I'm fine," she said.

"Is the victim dangerous?" the dispatcher said urgently.

Charlotte hesitated. "I don't think so?"

"I'm sorry." The man rested his forehead on the decking, breathing heavily. "You all right?"

"I think so."

Sirens sounded in the distance.

"They're here," Charlotte said into the phone. "Thanks."

"I need to go." The man pushed himself to hands and knees unsteadily.

"You should probably stay and get some medical attention," Charlotte said.

"Can't." He wiped at his face with his sleeve, then rose to one knee, bracing himself as he swayed.

"Are you sure? They're almost here."

The pier was suddenly flooded with light as an ambulance and a police car converged upon them from different directions.

The man let out a rough breath and remained on one knee, apparently resigned to being questioned.

Men in blue uniforms jumped out of the back of the ambulance, and a policeman in a bulletproof vest jogged up.

"I'm fine." The man waved them away. "Little clumsy, that's all."

The policeman frowned at him. "Let 'em check you, sir. What's your name?"

"Ronan." He doubled over and coughed again, expelling a little more water.

"Have you been drinking or anything?" the policeman asked conversationally.

"Just water," Ronan rasped.

The policeman snorted. "Can I see your ID? Andy has the gurney out; hold on a sec and he'll get you settled."

"I'm fine," Ronan repeated, shivering.

Andy, the paramedic, held out a hand. "Sure, you're fine. But let me listen to your heart and lungs anyway. Fluid in the lungs can cause problems later. Take off your coat and shirt and we'll get you in a thermal blanket."

"I'm fine!" Ronan said again, this time with a twinge of annoyance in his voice. He rose to his feet with a hiss of pain.

"What hurts?"

"Nothing."

"Give it a rest, tough guy," the policeman muttered. "It won't kill you to let the guy do his job."

"My apologies," said Ronan. "Pray continue."

Andy rolled his eyes at the second EMT and stepped forward to help Ronan remove his coat.

"Good gravy, this coat is heavy," Andy huffed.

"It's not meant for swimming," Ronan said in a dry voice. He fumbled with the buttons on his shirt as his hands shook, and the other EMT pushed his hands out of the way as Andy wrapped a foil-lined blanket around his shoulders.

He submitted to their examination without further protest.

Andy frowned. "I'm getting a pulse of 38 bpm. How do you feel?"

"Fine. A bit chilly." Ronan added, "It's always low. Nothing to worry about."

Andy flashed a light in Ronan's eyes, examining how his pupils contracted, and Ronan winced.

"You work out a lot or something?" Andy pressed.

"Or something. Are you done yet?" Ronan pulled the blanket from his shoulders and attempted to hand it back.

The EMT pushed the blanket back at him. "Keep that on."

"You never gave me your ID," the policeman said.

"Perhaps it fell in the water."

EMTs and the policeman conferred a moment. Charlotte stepped closer, and the policeman's attention snapped to her.

"You made the call, didn't you?"

Charlotte nodded.

"You all right?" the policeman asked, his gaze flicking over her, to Ronan, and then back to her. He stepped closer and lowered his voice. "The dispatcher said you sounded frightened. What happened?"

She chewed her lip, acutely aware of the midnight silence that enfolded them, so deep it seemed to swallow the faint lap of the water against the shore. Ronan's eyes were not on her, but she knew he was listening for her reply. "Nothing much. I just startled him, that's all."

The officer studied her face and then nodded. "You parked around here?" At her assent, he said, "How about I walk you to your car while Andy and Jeff finish checking out the swimmer?"

Charlotte hesitated. "Well, what about him then?" The icy breeze gusted, cutting through her coat, and she shivered.

"You have someplace to go?" the officer called to Ronan.

"I'll be fine," he said in a low voice.

"We'll get him home. Or to his car. Or the shelter downtown, if necessary."

Her hair blew into her face, and she brushed at it with trembling fingers. "I'll wait," she said uncertainly.

In a few more minutes, the men were arguing about where they were going to take Ronan, who stood, stony-faced, with the metallic blanket wrapped around his shoulders.

Finally, he said, "Am I being detained?"

"No, you're being taken to a shelter."

"No, I'm not," he said in a firm voice. "If I'm not being detained, I am free to leave, am I not?"

The officer sighed heavily. "Be reasonable. It's 29 degrees and dropping. I don't want to find you frozen into a popsicle on some park bench tomorrow. The shelter on Hickory has a bed open. I'll give you a ride and buy you a hamburger on the way there if you don't have a place to go."

A muscle in Ronan's jaw twitched, and he ground out, "Thank you, but *no, thank you*. I have a commitment I must honor. Shall I keep your blanket or give it back?"

The officer's eyes narrowed. "Bring it back tomorrow."

Ronan dropped his chin in a strangely formal gesture that reminded Charlotte of a bow. "I will."

Charlotte watched the EMTs load the gurney back into the ambulance and the vehicle drive away, followed by the police car.

When she looked back, Ronan was almost out of sight, and she jogged toward him.

"Are you all right?" she asked.

"Fine."

She raised an eyebrow, and he muttered, "Ankle's a bit sore. It'll be fine."

She glanced over her shoulder to see the police car's taillights disappear around a corner. They were alone.

The icy wind hissed through the bare branches above them. Ronan sat on an iron bench and hunched forward, wrapping the blanket more tightly around his shoulders. "You'd best get home," he murmured. "It's a bit chilly, and you probably have family in town for the holiday."

Charlotte stood a few feet away, feeling awkward and unsure of what to say. "Actually no. My family's in Texas, and I didn't have enough time off to make the trip."

He glanced up at her. "Alone for Christmas?" His voice had a strange, tight tone, and she couldn't tell whether he was sympathetic or mocking.

She cleared her throat. "Yeah. I mean, it's not what I wanted, but my dad just started a new job so he doesn't have time off either. Even if I ponied up the six hundred bucks I can't afford for a plane ticket, I wouldn't get to see them as much as I'd like. So we're saving our time for a week in the summer."

"Lonely?" he said abruptly.

"A bit." Her voice shook. Perhaps it was merely that she was shivering. Yes, that was definitely it. "So you didn't want to go to the shelter. I can give you a ride to a hotel or something if you need it."

"'s all right." His voice was nearly inaudible. "I don't have anywhere to be at the moment."

"You *lied* to them? It's Christmas! It's freezing! You'll die out here soaking wet!"

"I'm fine." He didn't look at her. "I'm meeting my… a friend… tomorrow. Close by."

"If you're that desperate to stay out of a shelter, you can sleep in my living room for tonight."

He glanced up then. "You'd let a sopping wet stranger sleep in your living room? I thought you were more cautious than that." His voice shook and he hunched forward, shivering.

"Will you promise to be a perfect gentleman?" she asked archly. If he were the type to take advantage of a woman, last night would have been a good opportunity. He could probably be trusted.

The silence drew out, broken only by the sound of the wavelets splashing against the pier and the wind rushing over the water and through the trees.

"You have my word," he said at last. "But I'll be gone before you wake. And I will offer appropriate recompense for your hospitality."

Charlotte blinked. "What recompense are you talking about? I don't run a bed and breakfast. It's just a night on my couch."

Ronan stood, not putting weight on his right foot. "Indeed." He smiled down at her, and she realized with a rush of nerves that he was taller and more intimidating than she'd realized.

She took an involuntary step back, and he frowned faintly. "Do I frighten you?"

"No! No. I um… my car's about a block that way." She started off briskly, hoping to regain a sense of equilibrium.

After a moment, she realized he wasn't at her side, and turned to see him limping some ten steps behind, carrying the still-dripping greatcoat. "I'm sorry," she cried softly.

At last, after a flight of seven concrete steps and a painful walk uphill, they reached her car in the law office parking lot. She unlocked the trunk, where they stashed the coat, then his door. He wrapped the blanket around his shoulders more tightly before maneuvering into the vehicle as she climbed in her own side.

Getting out of the icy wind was an immense relief. Again, blissfully warm air poured out of the vents almost immediately.

"Thank you," Ronan murmured. "Why are you doing this?"

She turned onto King Street and then south on Highway 1. "It seemed like the right thing to do." He was looking at her out of the corner of his eye, his lips turned slightly upward in a smile she could not interpret, as if he were thinking something amusing about her.

"You're making me uncomfortable," she said at last. "You're staring at me."

He blinked and shook himself. "My apologies." He turned to look out the window. "I haven't seen many..." He stopped, as if thinking better of the words. "Your beauty disarmed me, and I forgot my manners."

She rolled her eyes, imagining he was mocking her in a charming, albeit juvenile, way. "I'm sure," she murmured. She had the vague sense, then, that she had offended him somehow, but he said nothing else.

A short while later, she pulled the car into the reserved spot in front of her townhouse. "Here we are." She hurried forward to unlock the door, and he limped after her.

Inside, he stood wrapped in the thermal blanket as she hurried around, second-guessing her impulsive decision to have a stranger sleep on her couch.

"Would you like a shower? The bathroom's just up there." She pointed up the stairs, and he frowned at them grimly.

"I should." But he did not move.

"Actually, why don't you just sit down and rest your ankle?"

He hesitated, then grimaced as he limped painfully to the couch. "All right."

"I could make you hot tea or something to help you warm up."

"Thank you." The words were nearly inaudible.

She turned on the gas fireplace, put a mug of water in the microwave, and then went to him. "May I see it?"

He blinked at her slowly, and for the first time she realized how extraordinary his eyes were. The outer edge of each iris was a deep brown surrounding clear green-gold so intense that for a moment she couldn't think at all.

"I um… can you take off your shoe?" she said softly.

His hands were shaking, and he fumbled with the laces so badly that she pushed his hands out of the way and fought with the knots herself. The damp edge of his trousers felt icy against the back of her fingers. She loosened the laces and carefully tugged the shoe off, biting her lip at Ronan's hiss of pain. His sock was beige with a faint diamond pattern, and she peeled that off too, one hand on the sock and the other steadying his foot.

When she glanced up at him, he smiled faintly, his lips a bloodless white. "See? It's not so bad."

"Liar," she murmured, glancing back at his foot. Purple had blossomed under his pale skin, spreading around his ankle and down into his foot.

"It'll be fine." He leaned back into the couch with a deep sigh. "Thank you for your hospitality."

Charlotte retrieved the mug of steaming water and filled an infuser with her current favorite tea, a light jasmine white tea with no caffeine. From the vantage point of the kitchen, she could see the blanket bunched around his neck and his dark hair. She let the tea steep for a moment, then brought it to him, the infuser still in the water.

"It's not done yet, but if you just want the warmth…" Her voice trailed away as she realized his head drooped forward in sleep.

She took a deep breath and let it out slowly, wondering what she should do. Her phone buzzed, and she pulled it out to see a string of messages from Heather.

How'd it go?

Hey, tell me you're in your car heading home now.

Buzz. Check your phone.

I'm getting worried. Answer me.

Answer your phone.

If I don't hear from you in the next five minutes, I'm calling the cops.

She hurriedly sent a message back. *I'm fine. Long story. Guy is asleep on my couch. Name is Ronan.*

He's asleep on your couch?! No. You're kidding. Right?!

Not kidding. Sprained his ankle or something, was going to sleep on a park bench. I don't even know. I have a lock on my bedroom door and will sleep with my phone under my pillow. Pretty sure he's not a rapist or axe murderer, though.

Kick him out! Or go next door and crash on Lori's couch. Or Demetria's. This is not smart, Charlotte.

I know. But I prayed about it while the EMTs were checking him out. I think it'll be fine.

If I roll my eyes any harder, they'll fall out. Text me in the morning.

Sure.

Charlotte had the sudden urge to take a picture of Ronan and send it to Heather. She framed the shot on her phone screen, then caught herself; it was more than a little creepy to take a picture of a sleeping stranger, no matter how gorgeous he was. She winced and put the phone down, only to see Ronan regarding her steadily.

"I…" Her cheeks heated. "I… Here's your tea." She gestured toward the mug, her hand trembling.

He studied her a moment longer, then picked up the tea and sipped it. "Thank you."

She found an extra blanket in the closet and brought it to him. "I'm going to get ready for bed. Goodnight." Then she frowned. "Are you hungry or anything?"

He smiled, and the warmth in his eyes took her breath away. "You've done more than enough. Good night, Charlotte."

She locked the bathroom door behind her and showered. The steady rush of hot water through her hair and over her shoulders soothed her lingering chill.

As she stepped out of the bathroom, she glanced down the stairs and noted that Ronan was still on the couch, then stepped into her bedroom with a sigh. The sheets felt heavenly against her skin, and a comfortable drowsiness settled over her.

Then she lay awake, her eyes closed, turning the odd evening over and over in her mind.

She must have drifted asleep eventually, because she woke with a start.

The morning light spilled silver-blue across her white quilt.

A sound so soft she might have imagined it caught her ear, and she listened, hearing only her heartbeat and the silence of an empty apartment.

She dressed and hurried downstairs.

ON THE FIRST DAY OF CHRISTMAS

C harlotte's living room was empty, with no sign of her overnight guest other than a folded blanket at the end of the sofa. She chewed her lip, and then opened the front door. Snow blanketed the three steps to the sidewalk. Uneven footsteps led away from her door, down the short street, and across the lawn at the end of her row of townhouses.

She pulled on her coat, hat, boots, and gloves, and followed the trail.

Ronan's footsteps were uneven, but he had walked nearly two miles, weaving through the neighborhood and out the back, around the duckpond, over the stream, and into a stretch of forest on the other side.

Twelve Days of (Faerie) Christmas

The branches above her creaked in the morning stillness. The snow crunched beneath her boots.

He leaned heavily against a tree trunk some distance ahead of her, the thermal blanket still wrapped around his shoulders.

As she watched, he let himself down to sit leaning against the trunk.

Charlotte looked around, seeing no one else.

She stood irresolutely for another minute, then continued forward until she reached him. "Why are you sitting in the snow?"

He reached out and gathered a double handful of snow, then rubbed it roughly over his face with shaking hands. "I'm waiting," he rasped.

She squatted beside him, and he looked down.

"I'm fine," he muttered. "Just waiting."

"For what?"

He didn't answer, staring bleakly across the snow.

"What are you waiting for?" she asked again.

He glanced at her, then away. Snow drifted down on them, catching on his hair and eyelashes and stinging her cheeks. "I said I'd be gone before you woke."

"Don't you think it's a bit melodramatic to freeze to death just to keep a promise made in haste? Do you really think I'd begrudge you a few more hours in my living room while you figure out what to do next?"

He licked his lips, then looked at her again with glassy eyes. "Not at all melodramatic. I keep my word."

She snapped, "You said you were meeting a friend! I don't see anyone here, and I don't want to be responsible if you die of hypothermia!"

He winced and turned his face away. He sagged against the tree trunk, and his grip on the thermal blanket around his shoulders loosened.

"Hey! Stay with me. Either you come back and warm up on my couch, or I'll call the police and you can spend the night in a shelter or something. You're not sleeping here."

His head lolled back against the trunk. His eyes were closed.

"Stupid! Stupid stupid stupid!" Charlotte pulled out her phone and began to dial, her fingers trembling.

"Stop!" Someone pulled the phone from her hand.

A man knelt beside Ronan. He held her phone in one hand, out of her reach, and used the thumb of his other hand to pull back Ronan's eyelids to examine his pupils. He felt for Ronan's pulse in his neck, frowning.

"What happened to him?" he said abruptly.

"Who are you?" Charlotte replied.

The man looked up at her with bright eyes of such a pale blue they almost appeared silver. "That is none of your concern. Answer the question, if you please."

He was slim and young, perhaps in his early twenties. His hair was long, white-blond, and rebelliously spiked, and he wore a long, dark coat over a close-fitting dress shirt. He pulled the thermal blanket from around Ronan's shoulders and flicked up, letting it flatten like a picnic blanket. He lifted Ronan onto it, apparently untroubled by the larger man's weight, and then examined him from head to foot. He unbuttoned Ronan's shirt, his lips wrinkling as he uncovered a strange array of bruises.

"What are those?" Charlotte whispered. The bruises were circular, with diameters from half an inch to nearly two inches; each circle was a livid purple around the out-side and a fading red in the center.

The man leaned closer, gingerly pressing against the bruised skin from the outside of one circle toward the center. The pressure revealed that in the very center of the circle was a puncture. He hissed through his teeth. "Venom. I wish… never mind."

He leaned close to Ronan's face and murmured something.

The older man woke with a strained gasp, then rasped, "Took you a while, Cormac."

"You could have called." The man continued his ex-amination. "Anything else you'd like to tell me?"

Ronan rolled his eyes, then caught sight of Charlotte kneeling wide-eyed nearby. "I left you a gift."

The younger man reached Ronan's injured ankle and his eyes widened. "You stubborn…" He explored the injury with careful fingers, pulling Ronan's sock down to see the bruising that extended into his shoe and up his shin.

"What gift?" Charlotte asked.

A gasp of pain answered her. The man pressed both hands hard against Ronan's injured ankle, then wrapped his right hand around the top of his foot and pulled downward, producing a muffled crack.

"Stop!" Charlotte cried.

The man ignored her, his eyes narrowed as he tight-ened his grip. Ronan's back arched in pain. Charlotte shoved the man off-balance, and he let go.

Ronan gasped, "Thanks."

"Leave him alone!" Charlotte shouted. "What's wrong with you?"

The man's silver eyes glinted. "Is that how it is?"

"Are you done?" Ronan gritted.

"Near enough," Cormac said cheerfully. He stood gracefully, and Charlotte took an unconscious step back. He was, she realized, dangerously, *terrifyingly* beautiful. He was slim and scarcely taller than her own petite five foot three, but he seemed larger, somehow, as if the very air bowed before him. His quicksilver eyes laughed as she tried to gather her thoughts. "A gift, Ronan? Moving fast, I see."

His sharp grin widened as Ronan groaned, "Just help me up, would you? Stop harassing the poor girl."

Cormac clasped Ronan's hand and pulled him to his feet, steadying his elbow with the other hand. "You could do worse. I see fire in her." He grinned at Charlotte's narrowed eyes. "Forgive me. I speak too freely; such a compliment is not always taken as it is meant."

Ronan slumped sideways; Cormac slid his arm around the larger man's waist and pulled Ronan's arm around his own shoulders, supporting his weight.

Cormac glanced at Charlotte. "Be well. I owe you a debt for your service to my friend."

Then he pulled Ronan behind the nearest tree and they were gone.

Charlotte blinked and looked behind the tree.

"That's more than a little disconcerting," she muttered. The woods were bright with morning sunlight reflected off the snow. There was little underbrush; the 'forest' was only a strip of trees a hundred yards wide between upscale suburban neighborhoods. She wandered around for a while, looking for footprints in the snow, and grew increasingly confused when she found no departing prints.

The men had simply vanished.

Birdsong carried in the still air as Charlotte walked back home. How could two men vanish into thin air?

She unlocked her front door and stepped inside, quickly shedding her jacket, hat, boots, and gloves. Ronan had said he'd left her a gift, but at first she saw nothing unusual.

A small potted tree stood near the sliding door to her patio, covered in deep green oblong leaves. A bird perched on the largest branch, peering out at her with one dark eye.

"What are you doing here?" Charlotte asked. "And *how* did you get here?"

Ronan had left her a plant? And a *bird*?

It was a pear tree. Half-hidden in the leaves, she found three golden pears. Wasn't the tree too small to bear fruit? She couldn't help smiling as she bent to examine one of the pears. Its fresh, sweet scent made her think of summer picnics, bright sunlight glinting on a pond, walnuts on a salad of exotic greens.

The bird fluttered its wings and studied her with bright black eyes.

Charlotte spent the day reading by the fire, first with coffee and later with hot chocolate.

On the Second Day of Christmas

Sunlight streamed in through the window and across her bed, warming her toes through the comforter. Charlotte sighed in contentment and snuggled deeper into bed. A knock brought her to sudden wakefulness. She stumbled from bed and shoved her arms through the sleeves of her fuzzy pink bathrobe, then skipped down the stairs and across the living room to the front door.

She opened the door a crack, expecting to find a box from her parents on the doorstep.

Instead, Ronan smiled. "I didn't mean to wake you. Forgive me."

Her face heated. "I... it's all right. Do you want to come in?"

"No! No, that's all right. I just came to say thank you for… you know." He held out a slim glass vase with a single, elegant flower.

"It's beautiful," she whispered. The calla lily was so white it seemed to nearly glow in the early morning light. She took the vase from him carefully.

He shifted, and she realized he was leaning heavily on a cane.

"Oh! Come in and sit down."

She pushed the storm door open further, surprised at her impulsive invitation.

He licked his lips and glanced over his shoulder, then limped inside.

"I'll get coffee started. Sit down while you wait? I can make breakfast in a bit, if you want. I um… well, I guess I have breakfast ingredients? Maybe cereal?"

"Thank you." His gaze rested on her in an appraising manner, and she felt as if she ought to stand up straighter. She wished she'd at least washed her face and brushed her teeth before he'd knocked.

She flushed and turned away. What right did he have to look so polished at this time of morning? "Bother!" she muttered under her breath. She filled the pot with water and turned on the burner. Then she yanked open the refrigerator and pulled out the carton of white mocha creamer, poured some half and half into a miniature pitcher, and set them both near the French press.

"I'm going to get dressed. I'll be back in a minute." She fled up the stairs to her bedroom.

Several minutes later, face washed, teeth brushed, and dressed in jeans and a sweater, she descended the stairs to find Ronan looking out the window. His fingers flexed on the head of his cane.

"You should sit down," she offered. "How's your ankle?"

"Fine," he said. He glanced down the street, then turned to face her with a polite smile. "I thank you again for your kindness."

She flushed. "You're welcome. The water's probably hot."

He blinked. "What?"

"For the coffee?" She ducked into her little kitchen and poured the hot water into the French press, glancing at him through her bangs.

He looked outside again.

"It will be ready in a minute." When he didn't answer, she said, "Is something wrong?"

"Not yet," he muttered. From inside his coat he produced two birds that hopped from his hand to the windowsill, where they settled against each other with much soft cooing and rustling of feathers.

Charlotte cleared her throat. "Why are there two birds on the window sill?"

He glanced over his shoulder at her, his faint, worried expression deepening. "I should go." He jerked his chin toward the door and the birds flapped to his shoulders. He leaned heavily on the cane as he limped around the sofa, the birds swaying with each step.

At the door he turned and met her gaze. "Forgive me for intruding. Farewell." He bowed slightly, and then opened the door.

A snap of something sent him stumbling backward, and the birds launched off his shoulders.

He hissed sharply through his teeth as he straightened. "Stay back," he growled.

"What is it?"

A screech split the air.

A snake-like head struck at Ronan, who slashed at it with a sword. Charlotte wondered where both the monster and the sword had come from but was distracted by the deafening screeching and flapping of wings and cooing.

Then the foyer was empty but for Ronan leaning against her coat closet door with a long, narrow sword in one hand and a bird on his head. "Do you mind?" he growled, and swiped at it with one hand. It fluttered its wings irritably and cooed at him.

"What was that?" Charlotte asked. Her voice shook, and she took a tremulous breath. "Are you all right?"

"I'm fine." Ronan straightened with a pained hiss. He bent to slip the sword back into the cane, then leaned against the wall, his jaw tight.

He looked… well, a bit worse for wear. A razor-thin scratch across his temple dripped blood down one cheek; another crossed the back of his right hand.

"You're bleeding."

He glanced at her. "Really? Where?"

Charlotte gestured at her cheek, and he swiped his hand experimentally across his cheek, leaving his palm streaked with blood.

He gave the other bird, now perched on the back of the sofa, a dirty look. Then, in a perfectly reasonable voice, he said to Charlotte, "That was an unpleasantness you're unlikely to meet again. I'll leave the turtledoves with you for a week or so, just in case. The creature doesn't like them." He glanced at his hand, then wiped again at the blood dripping down his face. "Do you mind if I…"

"Oh! Oh, yes. Sorry." Charlotte, flustered, gestured at the sink.

He leaned heavily on his cane as he limped around the counter. She turned on the water and stepped back. He leaned the cane against his leg, then bent to splash water on his face; she handed him a hand towel, and when he blotted his face with it, the wound quickly began bleeding again. He sighed and pressed the towel to his temple. "I'm sorry," he said in a low voice. "I just meant… I was just bringing you a flower."

Charlotte chewed her lip, then offered, "Go sit down. The coffee's ready. Creamer or just half and half? Sugar?"

A spark of relief brightened his expression. "I… don't know. I've never had coffee before."

She blinked. "Never?"

"Is it common?" He pulled the towel from his head and touched the wound experimentally with one finger, only to discover it was still bleeding freely. "Think you could be a little more careful?" he muttered in the bird's general direction. He wrapped the towel tightly around his wounded hand while he limped to her little dining table, carefully lowered himself into a chair, and then renewed pressure on the head wound.

"Well, yes, many people drink coffee." If he hadn't had it before, he'd probably prefer lots of cream and sugar. She poured a generous amount of creamer into his mug, and a slightly lesser amount into her own. "I can make us eggs and toast. How many eggs do you want?"

"I don't mean to impose."

She glanced at him. He was looking across the room at her pear tree and the bird in it with a strange expression.

"Three eggs sound good?" she ventured. After starting the toaster, she scrambled the eggs and put them on plates, then buttered the toast. "Here," she said quietly, sliding the plate in front of him.

He blinked, as if coming back from distant thoughts. "Thank you," he murmured.

"Is it still bleeding?"

He lowered the towel and tentatively brushed a finger over the cut. "I think it's stopped."

Charlotte leaned forward, examining the wound. "What did it?" The cut was as fine as if done by a scalpel, and the pressure of the towel had already pressed the edges together. Fresh blood beaded up in several spots, but the other areas appeared to be sealed. "It looks like it will heal without a scar."

He flashed a quick, careless grin. "I don't doubt it. I only regret the discomfort it caused you." Then he glanced at the towel. "And I believe I owe you a small cloth of some sort."

She blinked at him. "It's a dish towel. I wanted a new one anyway. Don't worry about it." She hesitated, then bowed her head to pray quickly before the meal.

When she raised her head, Ronan also had his head bowed, his expression solemn. She waited while he finished, and when he raised his head, his eyes gleamed with pleasure. But he said nothing until she said, "You didn't answer my question."

He raised his eyebrows, but she had the distinct impression that he remembered the question and was merely avoiding it.

"What cut you?"

He studied her contemplatively a moment, then said, "An answer for an answer? I have questions as well."

"I suppose." Why did he seem so cautious, as if she were dangerous?

A muscle twitched in his jaw, and he said carefully, "One of the turtledoves. It was an accident."

"With its claws?" She frowned.

"It's my turn to ask a question." His eyes glinted. "How do you know of magic? I thought humans knew nothing of Faerie, yet you have a magic pear tree *and* a partridge."

She stared at him, her breakfast forgotten. "*You* left it in my living room yesterday when you tried to freeze yourself in the park!"

He tilted his head, dark eyes sweeping over her and back to her face. "I left you a potted plant! I didn't specify the species, and the partridge... well, I didn't ask for an extra bird. That came on its own." The muscle in his jaw twitched again, and he said tensely, "Did you change my magic? Don't you know the implications of that?"

She blinked. "Of course I didn't! And that's two questions, but I'll answer them both. I don't know what implications you're talking about."

He winced. "That was unfair. Don't answer a question out of turn, if you please."

Charlotte huffed in irritation, half-feigned and half-genuine. "Whyever not? I'm trying to be agreeable!"

"There are repercussions!" He pressed his lips together in dismay, then sighed. "I've been discourteous. Will you forgive me?"

Charlotte hesitated, counting questions, then nodded. "Yes, of course. Will you eat your breakfast, please?"

Ronan blinked, then his lips twitched into a surprised smile. "Are you always so kind to disconcerting strangers who show up at your door too early in the morning?"

"I've never had a disconcerting stranger show up at my door so early before, but you don't strike me as someone I need to fear. Who was your friend yesterday?"

His eyes gleamed with understanding, but he hesitated. "Perhaps you could call him a work associate, quite a bit higher in the power structure. Very close to the top, indeed. We've been friends for years, despite my humble status. You liked him?"

"He seemed nice enough, I suppose. How'd you disappear so quickly?"

He blinked, surprised by her disinterest in his friend. "He opened a door and we went through it." He took the first sip of his coffee and froze, holding it in his mouth. He frowned, considered the taste, then swallowed it. "What an odd beverage. Do you drink it often?"

"Pretty much every morning. Do you like it?" He had a faintly disgruntled look on his face, and she tried not to laugh at him.

"I'm not sure." He peered in the cup, then glanced up at her. "Do you have another question?"

She grinned at him, and his eyes sparkled in response. "How bad is your ankle?"

"A couple broken bones. It's healing fast." He took a bite of eggs. "This is delicious. Quite strange, but delicious. Have you another question?"

47

"What pulled you under the water?"

His expression darkened. "Nothing you need worry about. I handled it." He hesitated, then, apparently feeling that he ought to give a real answer, he muttered, "A young kraken. They start out small, you know. It came through just before I got there." He sighed heavily, and said, "I'm sorry about pulling the knife on you." He glanced up to meet her gaze. "Will you…"

"I already did."

His eyes flickered with relief.

"Do you have a sword in your cane?"

"Yes. It seemed prudent. Do you have any other questions?" he said softly.

"But you *do* really need the cane?"

"Indeed."

She studied his face across the table, the faint lines of weariness beside his eyes and the tightness of his lips. "I think I'm done with this game."

"Agreed."

They finished eating in near silence. Several minutes later, Ronan sat back with a contented sigh. "That was a delightful repast. Thank you."

He stood, bracing himself on the table with one hand while he got the cane into position. He limped to the pear tree and bent to study it, glancing from the leaves to Charlotte and back again. The partridge eyed him and chirruped agreeably, and he absently rubbed it on the head with one finger.

At last he said, "Huh. Interesting."

"What's interesting?"

"I don't know yet." He straightened. "You can eat the pears, if you like."

"What about… I mean, will the bird make messes? Do I need to feed it?"

He blinked. "It wouldn't be much of a gift if it did, would it?" He sounded vaguely offended. "It's self-contained. The partridge eats the pears and needs nothing else. The pears are fed by the partridge."

When she said nothing else, he said, a trifle stiffly, "Good day to you." He winced as he turned to limp toward the door.

"Good day," she said softly as he strode outside.

He must not have heard her, for he didn't look at her as he closed the door behind himself.

The two turtledoves cooed atop the bookshelf beside the fireplace. She watched surreptitiously out the window as he limped down the sidewalk. Snow had begun falling again, and it caught in his hair, glittering like diamonds.

On the Third Day of Christmas

A tap tap tapping woke Charlotte a few minutes before her alarm sounded. She stared at the ceiling, wondering blearily if Ronan was bringing her another flower, and if some "unpleasantness" was going to follow.

She sighed at her own uncharitable thoughts. In truth, she was concerned rather than annoyed, with an unpleasant twist in her belly when she thought of him limping off into the snow. She should have asked him if he needed a ride to the emergency room, or at least a painkiller.

The tap tap tapping sounded again, more insistently. She dressed hurriedly and ran to open the door.

Three hens clucked disapprovingly at her and scuttled past her feet into her living room, where they ran excitedly in circles, clucking and chirruping.

In French.

She sighed and picked up the box that had apparently been sitting on the top step since the night before.

Inside, she crossed her arms and glared at the hens, which settled into a line on the hearth and clucked at each other under their breath for a moment, then looked back at her in unison.

"Why are you here?" she exclaimed.

There was much clucking and rustling of feathers. *Ronan nous a donné des ordres.*[1]

Charlotte didn't speak French, but she thought she picked out Ronan's name. "Ronan sent you?" she squeaked. "Why?"

They fluttered their wings and shuffled their feet, clucking softly.

She buried her face in her hands.

It was Sunday, and she'd promised Jim she'd work a few hours in the afternoon to help with that case. But the morning was reserved for church, and she enjoyed it every bit as much as usual. She wanted to stay and chat, but the singles were all going out to a restaurant that she knew would be slow. So she hugged her friends and said goodbye.

While driving to work, she had visions of more birds in her apartment, bird messes on the counters and floors, feathers on her pillows and wafting over the stove as she cooked. It was ridiculous! Ronan would have to take them back. What could she possibly want with more birds?

---

[1] *Ronan gave us orders.*

By the time she reached the office, she wavered between righteous irritation and giggles at the absurdity of it.

She sent a series of texts to Heather while waiting for the coffee to brew.

How's the family? Ronan and I had breakfast yesterday. He probably needs to see a doc about his ankle. Weirdness ensues every time I see him. My apartment is filled with birds. When he's not being cagey, he's pretty charming, though. Except for the birds. I don't really need any more birds.

Jim was already in his office with the door closed.

She poured herself a cup of coffee and knocked on his door. "Coffee's hot."

A muffled acknowledgment came through the door, and she strode to her desk. Normally the office would be relaxed between Christmas and New Years, but the big case was taking all their time. While awaiting Jim's direction, she caught up on the accounting.

Jim's door finally opened and heard him step into their tiny kitchen. She took a deep breath and followed him.

"How's it going?" she asked.

He glanced at her, then back at the coffee. "Discovery ends Friday. We have nothing useful. I know Swanson's hiding the evidence but I don't have a way to prove it." He took a swig of coffee and closed his eyes. "His attorney is crooked and slippery as a snake, and Perry's going to get twenty to life if we can't get something useful by Friday. And there's *nothing* I can find in the paperwork to prove it beyond a reasonable doubt, even though it's obvious to anyone with the IQ of a turnip."

He rubbed both hands over his face and then through his hair, leaving the salt and pepper fluff in disarray. He sighed again. "Where's Heather?"

"On vacation. You approved it in November."

"Oh." He looked vaguely annoyed, though it was probably more at himself than Heather. "Help me look through the bank records, would you?"

"Sure."

He carried a box of paper to her desk, and she got started.

"Home again, home again," Charlotte murmured, prepared for a horrific mess as she opened her front door.

Stepping cautiously inside, she didn't see any evidence of bird poo or lost feathers. Perhaps the birds had at least gone on the kitchen linoleum rather than the living room carpet.

The living room was surprisingly clean. She glanced at the French hens suspiciously out of the corner of her eye as she noted the neatly arranged decorative pillows and spotless countertop. Hadn't she left her cereal bowl in the sink that morning?

She walked through each room and looked for hidden messes behind curtains and doors. The bookshelves were freshly dusted and her bed was made. Had she made her bed that morning? She couldn't remember. Ducking her head into the bathroom, she noted the new towels. They smelled faintly of lavender, and she narrowed her eyes. She liked lavender, certainly, but she didn't own a lavender sachet.

After going through every room, she flopped down on her sofa and studied the birds through narrowed eyes. "Did you clean my entire apartment?"

The hens clucked cheerfully to each other.

"Why?"

They shuffled their feet and stared at her, muttering and clucking in French. *Ronan nous a envoyé.*[2]

Charlotte threw her hands up in despair. "Ronan! Ronan and his birds! Is he coming back?"

She might have sworn they were laughing at her.

Voulez-vous qu'il le fasse? Oh, il sera ravi![3]

She glared at them. If she understood French, she'd probably be even more annoyed. Or perhaps worried.

She fixed a dinner of linguine with chicken and alfredo sauce from a jar. The hens didn't seem concerned by her choice of protein. She cooked enough for leftovers (or a guest) and lit the candle in the middle of the table.

After dinner (alone), she turned her attention to the box of gifts from her parents. Each of four smaller boxes was impeccably wrapped in textured white paper adorned with silver foiled snowflakes. Charlotte smiled, imagining her mother wrapping them at the kitchen table, her father dutifully handing her appropriately sized pieces of tape.

Received the package! Thank you! Should I open it tonight or tomorrow?

---

[2] *Ronan sent us.*
[3] *Do you want him to? Oh, he'll be delighted!*

Receiving no answer, she decided to wait until the next day. Her parents would want to hear her excitement as she opened each gift.

"Goodnight," she murmured to the birds as she went to bed.

They clucked softly in reply.

On the Fourth Day of Christmas

S
he nearly made it through breakfast before anything strange happened. As she picked up the last bite of toast, she heard an uproar of avian squawks outside.

"Oh no. No no no," she muttered. She yanked open the door to see four enormous black birds attacking a… what was that thing? Something with too many legs, scales, and a goat-like head topped by three horns, with tusks jutting from each side of its mouth.

She swallowed and watched from the relative safety of the doorway.

The birds shrieked in rage as the thing struck at them, diving and pecking with surgical precision at its eyes and ears. It screamed in response and swiped at them with huge clawed feet.

Twelve Days of (Faerie) Christmas

From the corner of her eye, Charlotte saw Ronan sprinting down the sidewalk, leaning hard on the cane but otherwise heedless of his wounded ankle. He slapped a bird out the creature's snapping jaws just before it was crushed and shoved his sword down the monster's throat, up to his bicep in razor-sharp teeth. The sword came out the back of the creature's head, and it closed his jaws on Ronan's upper arm as it writhed.

Then it exploded in a cloud of sparkles.

Ronan breathed heavily for a moment, his breath fogging in the frigid air. He clutched at his arm, wriggled his fingers and bent his elbow experimentally, then hopped toward the scabbard that would enable him to use the sword as a cane. He sheathed the sword and leaned on it a moment, looking at the black birds now settled in the cherry tree in Charlotte's tiny yard, waved an elegant salute to them, and took a step toward the street without acknowledging Charlotte.

The step must have hurt more than he'd expected, because she heard his hiss of pain from the doorway. He stopped, shoulders tense, head bowed, and gathered himself for a moment before taking another step.

She cleared her throat, and he paused, not looking at her.

"Would you like some help?"

His jaw worked, and finally he ground out, "I'm fine."

The wind gusted, cutting through her sweater, and she shivered. "Please come inside."

He sagged. "I'd rather not," he muttered. "It's... you're complicating things."

"Me?" Charlotte's voice cracked. "*I'm* complicating things? My life was predictable and pretty decent right up until I met you. Now my apartment is full of birds and a magic pear tree and I have monsters in my front yard!"

He covered his eyes with his left hand and sighed wearily. "Exactly."

"So let's make the best of it, shall we? You've probably done all sorts of damage to that ankle. I'll call Jim and tell him I'll be late."

His head dropped, and he pressed his lips together. Without conviction, he muttered, "I shouldn't."

"Why not? It's freezing cold! Don't be ridiculous."

"Why should I not be?" he snapped. "This whole situation is ridiculous. *Why* are there four colley birds in your tree? Why did you have a *tugann bás* in your yard?" He sighed. "Forgive me. I spoke unkindly and with poor courtesy. Bid me depart, and I will."

Charlotte's heart constricted at the weariness in his shoulders, and she said softly, "If I bid you come in and rest a moment, will you?"

He hesitated, then nodded reluctantly. "As you wish."

"Then yes. Do that, then." She considered darting to him and helping him limp to the patio and up the two stairs, but some sudden wisdom kept her back. Instead, she merely held the door open for him and stood aside as he made his way painfully across the yard, up the steps and across the tiny patio, and through the foyer.

"Sit on the sofa," she prompted, when he stood stiffly beside her dining table. "Would you like coffee? Or maybe hot chocolate?"

His gaze followed her. "Your drinks are strange to me. Choose as you will."

She decided on hot chocolate, heating the milk and glancing at him occasionally while she sent a quick text to Jim.

Minor crisis at home. I'll be in a few hours late. Sorry. Call if you need me.

He had, apparently without realizing it, relaxed a little against the back of the sofa rather than sitting bolt upright. He gazed at the pear tree through half-lowered eyelids and absently rubbed his right arm.

"How's your arm?" she asked.

He started. "Fine."

"Really? You don't look like it's fine." She tried for a teasing tone and was rewarded by an expression of surprised amusement.

"The jacket offered me some protection." He stopped rubbing his arm and clasped his hands in his lap. The position looked oddly formal.

There were punctures ringing the arm of his coat, and she said, "Did it break the skin? Break a bone?"

"Only minor punctures." He shrugged easily and shifted his attention to the pear tree. "Have you eaten any of the pears?"

"No."

He gave her a sidelong glance. "Truly?"

"Truly." The expression made her smile.

"The magic is wrapped around you like gossamer," he murmured, withdrawing to study her with his head tilted to one side. "And yet you know nothing of it."

She swallowed. "No. Why was there a monster in my yard this morning?"

He blinked. "It was drawn to… I should say no more."

"Don't you think I have a right to know?"

He frowned. "It's not a matter so much of a *right* but of *wisdom*, you see. Will it benefit you to know? I fear not. I think it will exacerbate matters. To tell you what I suspect tightens threads that I imagine you would prefer left loose." He sighed and rubbed his hand over his eyes. "Moreover, although I don't doubt your courage or your kindness, I doubt your desire to be… caught up… in the net that ensnared me so long ago." He smiled resignedly. "No matter. I have made a good life, and it is the richer for your generosity."

They sat in silence for some moments before Charlotte said, "Try the hot chocolate."

He sniffed it cautiously and glanced at her before he took a sip. His brows rose. "I like it," he said decisively.

Charlotte grinned. "I thought you might."

Her phone vibrated with a text from Jim. *Fine. Come when you can. Got more docs this morning.*

She sighed, chewing her lip.

"Is there a problem?"

"I need to go to work. Jim's working on an important case and he needs me." At Ronan's look of confusion, she explained, "He's a lawyer. We have a big case coming up, and he's pretty stressed about it." She looked down at her hands. "He's a good guy, really. But this has been rough on him."

Ronan glanced out the window before meeting her gaze. "The birds, silly as they might seem, are excellent guards. You'd leave their protection so willingly?"

Charlotte shrugged. "Well, why are monsters coming here? I might be safer at work."

His mouth twisted in a wry smile. "Your nonchalant courage is endearing. Did you mean it to be so?" There was a strange light in his eyes, as if he thought he might have caught her in some scheme.

"No, not at all. But I do need to go." She stood, and he stood with her, sucking in a pained breath as he did so. "I think you need to see a doctor," she said.

"No." His voice was firm.

"And you should probably stop walking on that ankle, don't you think?"

He snorted. "And then what? Sit in your living room until it heals? I think not. Look." He pulled up his trouser leg to show his ankle encased in what looked like grey mesh that disappeared into his wool sock and up his calf. "Cormac set the bone days ago and made me a splint."

She shrugged. "Suit yourself, then. Obviously my opinion isn't worth much."

She smiled to herself as the jibe hit home, then regretted it a moment later as he said in a stiff voice, "Your kindness is much appreciated, but I am subject to rules of which you are unaware. Pray forgive me for not assenting to your every wish. It is not entirely by my own choice."

Charlotte sighed. "I'm sorry. I was only trying to help. I went about it badly."

A muscle in Ronan's jaw twitched. "Much as it pains me to harass you further, I beg leave to accompany you to your workplace. I have no wish for you to be unprotected as matters escalate."

"What matters?"

He gave her a narrow, dangerous smile. "Matters which have thus far resulted in monsters, flocks of birds, a magic pear tree, and an unwelcome guest."

She cleared her throat. "Have I made you feel unwelcome? I didn't mean to. I mean, I'm a little discombobulated by everything. But..." she sighed. *Was* he welcome? Perhaps in other circumstances, she'd have been more delighted to have met him. His exaggerated courtesy was both amusing and charming, especially since it seemed so sincere. Not to mention how unsettlingly good-looking he was. Only the lines of weariness around his eyes and the sardonic set of his mouth kept him looking human.

His smile softened. "Perhaps I presumed too much. In truth, it pains me not a whit to be in your presence. Only the thought of your displeasure at my company made the request difficult."

The awkwardness faded, and in a few moments, they were in the car.

The ride was quiet. Ronan gazed out the window as if he'd never seen the city before, his eyes flashing from one sight to the next.

When they arrived, she led him up the two steps to the doorway and through little foyer and lobby, then through the hall to Jim's office. She knocked.

"Jim, I have a friend here with me."

He opened the door with a surprised "What?" and frowned at Charlotte and Ronan in turn. His frown deepened when he saw Ronan's cane. "Sit down, then. What brings you here?"

"Responsibilities," said Ronan.

Charlotte licked her lips. Mostly she'd let him come along because... well, she couldn't bear the thought of him limping away in the snow to go wherever he went. "I... um... well, I'm hoping to take him to the doctor later about his ankle. Anyway, he's a guest and I needed to be here, so I thought maybe he could help for a while."

Jim gave her a skeptical look. "Is that so?"

"Near enough," Ronan said quietly. "I'll be of assistance if I can be."

"Hmph. Well, I already put four boxes of papers at your desk, along with a list of people to call as possible witnesses."

"Let's work in the conference room. We can spread out a little more," Charlotte said.

Ronan frowned in dismay as she and Jim carried the boxes of papers to the conference room without his assistance.

"I'm ordering lunch soon. What do you want from Potbelly?" Jim asked.

"Roast beef." Charlotte glanced at Ronan, who looked back blankly. "Um, get two."

Charlotte explained what they were looking for, and then silence fell over the room as they began to page through the thousands of pages, one by one.

Half an hour later, Jim kicked her foot and flicked his eyes toward Ronan.

His head had drooped forward in sleep, left hand braced against the chair arm and right hand slack atop the papers he'd been reading. He looked pale; perhaps it was pain and exhaustion, or perhaps it was only the fluorescent lights.

"What's with him?" Jim whispered. "Who is he?"

Ronan's dark hair fell over his forehead, hiding his eyes, and Charlotte felt an odd sense of protectiveness as she considered how to answer. Jim was a friend, of course; not a close friend, exactly, but a good boss and a supremely *good* person, despite his irritability this month. She wanted to tell him the truth.

But what was the truth?

She imagined herself saying *He made my car run another couple miles to the gas station even though it was out of gas and left me his coat by accident, so I returned it the next day, and then he got attacked by a baby kraken and it broke his ankle, and since then we keep meeting either by chance or design, I'm not really sure which, and somehow I have lots of birds and a magic pear tree now. And monsters in my yard!*

She pressed a hand over her mouth and tried to keep in the slightly hysterical giggles. "He's a friend, I think, although we just met a few days ago. He broke his ankle doing something heroic. We keep running into each other, or maybe he's hanging around on purpose. I'm pretty sure he saved my life this morning." Her whisper sounded a little trembly with mingled laughter and long-held tears.

"From what?"

"A um... a thing in my yard."

Jim's frown deepened. "Where did he come from? Doesn't he have a job?"

Ronan cleared his throat and straightened. "I'm doing it, actually." He scrubbed a hand over his face, quite obviously trying to appear awake.

The awkward silence pressed upon Charlotte until the tears overtook the laughter, and she covered her mouth again, trying to steady her breathing.

It didn't work. Tears slid down her cheeks, and she caught her breath on a sob.

"What's this? Have I been more ill-spoken than usual?" Ronan scooted forward and peered at her face, looking almost comically chagrined. "Forgive me, though I know not what I've done."

She buried her face in her hands. "It's not your fault," she said, her voice muffled. "It's just... it's too much! There are birds in my apartment and kraken in the Potomac and... and... and *monsters* in my yard, and you don't seem bothered by them at all! And I *really* think you should see a doctor about your ankle, and I feel guilty every time you limp around and I don't drag you to the ER!"

Jim glanced between them with shrewd brown eyes. "Monsters?" he asked mildly.

Ronan smiled faintly, trying to meet Charlotte's gaze. "Nothing too terrible. They were all handled with minimal fanfare, wouldn't you agree?"

She swallowed and closed her eyes. "That's true. But... they *exist*! Isn't that enough to be terrifying?"

He gave a soft, low huff of laughter. "Not in the slightest. That's why I'm here." He caught her gaze and smiled, with a strange light in his eyes. "What do you think a doctor could do that Cormac hasn't already done for my ankle? And what guilt do you bear for my own obstinance in the face of your compassion? None at all."

Jim cleared his throat. "So... monsters?"

Ronan glanced at him. "Oh, they have names, of course, but to humans unfamiliar with their species, they may seem monstrous." Then he frowned. "I ought not speak of them to you, though."

The older man shifted in his chair. "I think you'll understand if I ask you to back away from Charlotte. Have you used any illegal substances recently?"

Ronan gave a lopsided smile, a hard edge in his eyes. "I think you'll understand if I refuse. I've assumed a certain responsibility for her protection, and while I have some small talent, it is far from capable of defending her at a distance. I'll distance myself at her insistence and nothing less."

"Stop it, please!" Charlotte cried. "Jim, I'm pretty sure he's not on drugs, so just... thank you, but don't. And," she turned to Ronan, "please understand how unreasonable it sounds to him. He hasn't seen the monsters in my yard or the birds."

"As you wish," murmured Ronan, with a courteous inclination of his head.

Jim stared at him with narrowed eyes. "Charlotte," he said in a low voice. "Are you in trouble?"

She took a deep, tremulous breath and let it out slowly. "Not any kind of trouble I think you can help with," she said at last. "I don't know why there are monsters in my yard, but..." She clenched her hands in her lap, examining her white knuckles and trying to steady her voice. "I trust him."

"All right." Jim's voice was flat, and she knew he doubted the wisdom of her words. She might have been irritated, but instead she was grateful. He was nearly twice her age; she didn't feel his interest in Ronan as intrusive, but rather as a fatherly sort of protectiveness.

"Thank you, Charlotte," Ronan said softly. His dark eyes sparked with a deep, hidden pleasure.

"Can I drop you somewhere?" Charlotte asked tentatively.

He looked thoughtful, then said, "The end of your street would be ideal. Thank you."

She shot him a skeptical look, and he smiled back easily.

She stopped the car at the intersection. He opened the door and maneuvered to the sidewalk over a thick ridge of snow pushed up by one of the many snow plows clearing the streets.

"Are you sure?" she asked.

"Yes, thank you." He bowed slightly. "Pleasant evening to you."

"The same to you."

Her mother called as she was pulling into her parking space. "You haven't opened your gifts yet, have you?"

"No, I knew you'd want to watch." Charlotte grinned, knowing her mother was pleased.

The boxes contained a soft pink scarf, three books she'd mentioned wanting to read, a gorgeous new sketchbook, and a magnificent set of oil pastels. "Thank you!" she cried. "Oh, thank you!"

Her father grinned. "Open the book."

She opened the sketchbook to see a receipt for a class at the Art League School near work, an extraordinary arts facility with distinguished instructors.

"You can choose the class," her father said. "There are several starting in February."

"Ah! This is amazing! Thank you, Mom and Dad!"

"You're welcome."

She would have told them about Ronan and the adventures of the last few days, but her mother said, "Andy, you should get to bed. You have to get up early tomorrow."

"I know. Goodnight, Charlotte. Love you." Her parents smiled at her.

"Goodnight. Love you," she said.

On the Fifth Day of Christmas

The scent of lavender and mint gently brought Charlotte to wakefulness, with a sense of rested comfort and relaxation.

She dressed, showered, and skipped downstairs to see the French hens fluffing their feathers with great aplomb on her hearth. They clucked merrily as they saw her, shivered their wings, and settled again, looking very satisfied with the world and with themselves.

Charlotte eyed her living room, noting details she had missed the day before. The spotlessly dusted mantel, bookshelves, and curtain rods gleamed. The curtains were now lightly scented with lavender and mint, no speck of dust marring the spotless fabric. "You vacuumed the curtains? *How*? You don't even have hands!"

Twelve Days of (Faerie) Christmas

The hens squawked quietly, and she knew they were laughing at her. *C'est magique ma chérie! Il n'y a aucune autre explication.*[4]

The absurdity of it started her giggling, and then she found that she could not stop. Breathless and teary-eyed with mirth, she stumbled to the couch and collapsed, giggling every time she looking toward the hens.

A knock sounded on the door, and she tried, with only minimal success, to stifle her laughter. She pulled the door open, still trying to compose herself, and found a small box.

She looked around.

There were no monsters of any sort. No birds except for the four ravens in the cherry tree, who appeared to be snoozing contentedly.

"Anything want to jump out at me?" she muttered.

She picked up the box and took it inside.

Deep etching in an intricate floral pattern covered the surface. Hiding within the design were several birds, their eyes picked out in gold. When she set it on the dining table, the two turtledoves flew to it and strutted around, looking pleased.

"Were you involved in this somehow?" she asked.

They cooed at her.

Pas de danger! Ils ont tous des bords tranchants. Ronan les a envoyés.[5]

She eyed the hens thoughtfully, wishing she'd understood more than Ronan's name.

"Ronan sent it, did he? Is it dangerous?"

Enfant stupide! Il t'enverrait son cœur s'il le pouvait, mais il y a des règles, tu sais.[6]

---

[4] *Magic, my darling! How else?*
[5] *Not likely! They're all sharp edges. Ronan sent them.*

Had one of them just called her stupid? It was too much, coming from a bird, and she dissolved into giggles again.

Maintenant vous l'avez fait! Elle aura encore dix minutes de rire![7]

Ce n'est pas de ma faute! C'est évident.[8]

Wiping tears of laughter from her eyes, she opened the box.

A set of five interlocked bangles rested on maroon velvet. Charlotte picked them up and realized it was some sort of puzzle bracelet. Each ring was etched with a pattern that might have been words of a language she did not recognize, and spiraled in and around a central space. She played with it for several minutes, growing more intrigued by the moment. What did it mean, and why had Ronan sent it to her?

Je ne m'attendais pas à ça! Oh, ça progresse bien.[9]

"It's rude to keep speaking in a language I don't understand," Charlotte muttered.

Pardon.[10]

She snorted, still focused on the rings. She couldn't seem to fit more than two together; every time she got a third nearly in place, the first one slipped away.

"Phooey. I have to go to work anyway." She set it aside, grabbed her purse, and started toward the door.

The hens erupted into agitated clucks and ran around the table legs and her own legs, nearly tripping

---

[6] *Silly child! He'd send you his heart if he could, but there are rules, you know.)*
[7] *Now you've done it! She'll be laughing for another ten minutes!)*
[8] *It's not my fault! It's obvious.*
[9] *I did not expect that! Oh, this is progressing well.*
[10] *Sorry.*

her. The two turtledoves cooed angrily at her; one launched itself at her head, nearly landing in her hair.

"What?!" she cried. "What now?"

One of the turtledoves landed at the box and poked at the bracelet with one foot as it continued cooing.

"Fine! I'll wear it. Is that what you want?"

The birds quieted the instant she slipped it over her wrist. The hens ruffled their feathers triumphantly and strutted back to their preferred location on the hearth, and the turtledoves lost interest in her completely and flew back to the top of the bookshelf.

She rolled her eyes.

Snow had fallen heavily overnight, and fog had settled in. The roads were congested, and the drive felt like inching through a cloud lit more by the taillights of the cars ahead than by the still-low sun. On mornings like these, she cultivated an attitude of patience and poise, deliberately ignoring the irritation of another driver cutting in front of her or hanging too close to her bumper.

Snow had begun falling again by the time she pulled into her parking space. Fat snowflakes drifted in her face as she opened the car door. They stuck to her eyelashes and concealed the patch of ice on the sidewalk that sent her reeling. She didn't fall, although there was a great deal of flailing and a surprised squawk.

She texted Heather while waiting for the coffee.

Ronan left me a puzzle bracelet this morning. I'm disconcerted by this for several reasons: I'm about 99.9% sure that everything he does is for more than one reason, so while it may be a gift, it's probably also something else. It's not a bird, which means things have escalated in some way I don't understand. I haven't seen him this morning, but he came by my house, which is either creepy or not weird at all. I'm not sure I can tell any more.

Heather responded: *I'm coming back late tomorrow. Be safe, ok?*

I'll try. The snow this morning is beautiful. Four inches!

Traffic not so much?

Ha. No, took me almost an hour to get to work. It's eleven miles.

Jim said from the doorway, "Texting up a storm, huh?"

She blushed. "Sorry. I was trying to catch Heather up on Ronan. And stuff."

"Huh." He got out a coffee mug and asked, "So where is he now?"

"I don't know."

"Where does he live?"

"I don't know."

He glanced at her. "What does he do?"

"Um…"

He sighed. "Look, I'm not trying to tell you what to do or anything. But… don't you think that's a little… odd? He'd never had a roast beef sandwich before! That's odd."

"I think…. I think he's from pretty far away." Charlotte frowned. "I should probably ask him."

After a long, unproductive day of looking through page after page after page of excruciatingly boring bank records, Charlotte waved at Jim as she left for the evening. She pulled her hat on before opening the door to the parking lot and stepping outside.

Twelve Days of (Faerie) Christmas

A shadow wafted from the bush beside the doorway and coiled closer with startling speed. No breeze ruffled her hair.

Charlotte froze, every nerve screaming in fear.

The shadow flowed up the step and darted toward her foot.

She screamed and swatted at it. Her bracelet tinkled merrily.

The shadow evaporated just as Jim threw open the door and collided with her. He steadied her with one hand while his gaze swept around the darkened parking lot. "What's wrong?" he barked.

Her breath came fast with fear. "There was…" From the corner of her eye, she saw Ronan hurry around the corner.

Jim saw him too. "You!" he snapped. "What are you doing here?"

"Are you all right?" Ronan asked her, ignoring Jim.

"What was it?" she cried. "Like a shadow that moved by itself."

Jim's skepticism washed over her in a wave. "Charlotte, if he's harassing you, we can get a restraining order tonight. You can stay with a friend, or I can put you up in a hotel with security if you want."

"It's not him. I don't know what it was, but it wasn't him."

Ronan reached the bottom of the steps; standing two steps higher, she was nearly eye-level with him. His eyes sparked with a bright, glorious relief as he said softly, "You're wearing the bracelet. Thank you."

"Actually it's like five bracelets as one."

"What?" His voice cracked, and his smile fell away, leaving a hunted expression. "Let me see it!"

She held out her arm and pulled her jacket back to show the bracelets around her wrist.

A muscle in his jaw twitched, and he examined the bracelets. His fingers brushed the skin of her wrist, and she felt a strange, uneasy flutter inside, as if some deep emotion had just been awakened. Then he pulled away. He pressed his fist to his lips, then raked his hand through his hair, leaving it disheveled in a way that Charlotte, to her own surprise, found utterly charming. "Well, now what?" he muttered. "I tried, didn't I?"

"Tried what?"

"To release you! The magic keeps changing and I can't…" He rubbed his hand over his face again, leaving his eyes covered. "I don't have much magic, you see." He looked up at her, his expression grim. "What magic I have is mine only inadvertently, as a result of being captive for so very long. And Cormac won't release you. I've begged him." His jaw tightened. "And in all my years of service, I've *never* begged him for anything else."

"Release me from what?" she whispered.

His jaw worked, and he glanced at the shadows behind him, then down at the ground.

"If you're going to talk, how about in the lobby?" Jim said.

Charlotte knew the suggestion wasn't entirely to bring them back into the warmth; it was also because he would be there, a short hallway and an open door away. That is, if he intended to step out of the room at all.

"All right. Thanks."

Ronan limped up the stairs. When they were inside, she offered him coffee, and he shook his head.

"Tea, maybe? Just to have something warm?"

He meant to refuse, but then relented. "Thank you."

Jim hovered awkwardly in the tiny kitchen while she made the tea. "Do you want me in there?"

"No, it's all right. Thanks though."

He steepled his fingers and pressed his fingertips together, frowning. "I'll be in my office, then. Door's open. Shout if you need me."

"Thanks."

Ronan was still standing in the center of the lobby when she returned.

"Sit down." She put the mug of tea on the end table. "So you'll explain it all now?"

His lips twisted in a sardonic smile. "*All*? No, not *all*. But a little." He looked down at the floor. "The bracelet was intended to be a charming bauble, signifying my gratitude and—" he cleared his throat "—affection. Yet somehow my gift became five rings that are still one bracelet. May I see it again?"

She held out her wrist, then began to pull off the bracelet.

"No! Please leave it on," he said hurriedly. He placed her hand palm down upon his own warm palm, and carefully turned her hand to examine the bracelets from different angles. If he hadn't been so focused, she might have thought it was some strange ploy to hold her hand. But his expression was entirely serious. There were dark shadows beneath his eyes, as if he hadn't slept in days, and his mouth was set in an unhappy line.

His brows lowered, and he let out a soft breath, with a strange, defeated, sick expression.

"What's wrong?" she asked finally.

He let her hand go with unexpected tenderness, as if he wanted to keep hold of it but didn't have the right. "Cormac's magic is wrapped up in this. Perhaps... perhaps I'm misinterpreting it. But I know his magic by now, and it's his magic threaded through those rings."

"What does that mean?" she whispered.

Ronan's jaw worked. "I don't... I shouldn't speculate."

"Aren't you friends? Why don't you ask him?"

He shot her a dark glance. "Yes, we're friends."

"Then ask him." She hesitated, then, softly, asked, "Where are you sleeping?"

"Oh, here and there." He drew back, and she imagined there was reluctance in the withdrawal.

"Here and there *where*? Where do you live?"

"Mostly there." He smiled faintly, his extraordinary eyes gleaming with humor. "I've been here a bit more the last few days."

"Where exactly is *there*? And *here*?"

"Faerie is there, of course, and here is self-explanatory—this portion of the human world."

She narrowed her eyes. "Faerie." It wasn't exactly that she didn't believe him; between the monsters, the magic pear tree, and the birds, it was hard to deny that something was a bit strange. "What is it like?"

He gave a soft huff of startled laughter. "Glorious, and dangerous, and never, *ever*, entirely familiar. The human world, despite my unfamiliarity with your foods and customs, feels like coming home."

She tried to deny the flutter inside at the way his lips curled, at the soft edges of his voice that reached her ears and wrapped around her like an embrace. "Should *I* talk to Cormac?" she asked. If she didn't stay focused, she'd end up in love with him, and then where would she be? "I don't think I like him, by the way. He laughed when you were in pain." She clamped her lips shut, quelling the sudden urge to fill up the silence with words.

Ronan laughed aloud. "Don't like him? Oh, he very much likes you." Her eyes widened, and he added, "He called you a sleeping ember, quietly burning with passion yet unreleased."

Her brows lowered. "Is that supposed to be a compliment?"

"From a faery? Sure it is." He frowned and glanced toward the hallway. "Your man Jim is listening, you know."

Charlotte covered a smile with her hand. Of course Jim was listening; he'd want to be prepared if she needed help. "I'm fine," she called softly.

Jim walked into the room, making no pretense of not having been eavesdropping. "All right. Time's up. I need to lock up."

"Thank you for the time," Ronan said courteously as he rose, wincing.

"So where are you staying?" Charlotte asked. "You're not sleeping on a park bench, are you?"

"Not exactly," Ronan said lightly. "I'm fine."

He didn't smell like he was sleeping in a park, but he did look pale and exhausted. She wondered whether he'd eaten since the sandwich lunch the day before. "Are you hungry?"

"I'm fine," he repeated.

She sighed, chewing her lip. "Look, if you're sleeping outside, why don't you sleep on my couch instead?" She winced, feeling as awkward as if she were propositioning him, which she was emphatically *not* doing. "It's so cold, and... and it's just wrong."

Jim gave a bark of startled, offended laughter. "Charlotte, are you sure that's wise?" he said. "Do as you wish, of course, but consider your safety, please."

Ronan stiffened, and the silence felt like the moment before lightning struck. "I'll thank you not to imply such things about my character," he said icily. "I'd rather be eviscerated by a griffin than offend her." The hand holding his cane was white-knuckled, and Charlotte had the terrifying feeling that he wished to prove his words with blood.

Jim stared at him with narrow eyes, then glanced at Charlotte. "Do whatever you want. I'll expect you in the morning."

"I'll be in," she said quietly.

The drive to Charlotte's townhouse was nearly silent. When the awkwardness was too fraught to bear, she said, "Don't be angry at him. He's just trying to look out for me."

"I know. Forgive me, please." His voice had a strained tone, and she glanced at him, but the streetlights and shadows flickering over his face didn't permit her to read his expression.

"Are you all right?" she asked.

"I'm fine."

Liar, she thought.

"Thank you," he said quietly as they pulled into her parking spot. "You're very kind."

The ravens, or colley birds, squawked softly from the cherry tree. He waved to them, the gesture both careless and graceful, and she wondered whether they were more intelligent than regular ravens. Well, of course they were… but how much? She waved to them too.

She led him up the steps and into the foyer, where the hens and turtledoves swarmed him, cooing and clucking and chirruping joyfully.

"Yes, hello, good evening, thank you. I'd like to walk without tripping, please? Do you mind? All right, out of the way, please, Sonia." He pushed one of the hens gently out of his way with one foot, then edged forward, careful not to kick them or step on any toes. "Yes, thank you, you're doing a magnificent job." He winced in mostly-feigned irritation as one of the turtledoves scrabbled for purchase in his hair.

"Go sit down," Charlotte said.

"Thank you." He made his way to a sofa and lowered himself into it with a stifled groan.

"I was going to make stir fry for dinner. Is that all right?"

"Whatever you wish." He rubbed both hands over his face and through his hair, temporarily dislodging the turtledove, which immediately hopped back to its preferred place on his head. He left his hands clasped behind his neck as he leaned back into the sofa. Then he straightened. "Should I help? I don't know how…" He sighed and looked down the floor, his hair standing up in wild disarray.

"It's not hard. I'll do it. Just rest your ankle."

From her vantage point in the kitchen, looking over the little granite peninsula, she saw the defeated look pass over his face.

Several minutes later, stirring cubes of chicken into minced garlic and oil and spices, she stole another glance at him. This time his head had fallen back against the cushions, and he was asleep.

One of the hens clucked softly, hopped up on the couch, and settled herself in his lap. The turtledoves perched by his head, cooing. The two other hens settled themselves on the arm of the couch; one snuggled into the crook of his arm.

She started some rice and, struck by a sudden thought, glanced at Ronan again. His coat was still buttoned, but the collar of his white shirt was stained with blood from his cut days before, and what she could see of his trousers was crusted with dried mud. Not to mention that his coat had been dunked in the Potomac River, which wasn't exactly pristine. She stepped outside, walked next door, and knocked.

A moment later, a tall young man opened the door. "Hey, Charlotte! What's up? Come on in." He opened the door wider, and his wife waved cheerily from where she was folding the laundry spread across the sofa.

"Hey, Jerome. I just have a quick, kind of strange request. I... um, well, I have a friend crashing on my couch. He doesn't have any clean clothes. Can he borrow a pair of sweatpants and a t-shirt or something?"

Jerome blinked. "Yeah, sure. Is everything ok?"

"Um... yes, I think so." She frowned a little. "I'm fine. It's just kind of a weird time, and he needs a place to stay for tonight."

Jerome motioned her in out of the flurrying snowflakes, and she waited while he picked up a folded pair of sweats and a black t-shirt with a large lion in white above the words *He's not a tame lion. But he's good.* "This work?" he asked, then plopped an enormous hoodie on top of the stack. "Here, take that too. You have our number if you need anything, right?"

"Yep, thanks."

"Call anytime," said Demetria. "Even if it's late."

"Thank you." She smiled, grateful for their friendship.

She stepped back inside quietly, seeing Ronan still asleep on the couch. At the sound of the door closing, he let out a long breath and sagged deeper into the cushions. The hens eyed her disapprovingly and muttered among themselves.

Charlotte checked the rice, and then began filling two plates. She made a salad of fresh spinach, walnuts, and dried cranberries, then filled tumblers with ice and water.

"Hey," she said softly. "Dinner's ready."

He snapped awake, half-rising with wide eyes before he realized where he was. "Sorry, what?"

"Dinner's ready." She gestured toward the table.

He stared at it blankly, then back at her for a moment in bleary-eyed confusion."I'm sorry. Dinner. Yes." He rubbed his face hard. "Right. Thank you." He found his cane and gestured gallantly for her to lead the way to the table.

"Is it hurting more?" Charlotte asked.

"It's all right. I'm just tired."

After the first bite, he said, "This is delicious. Thank you," and she nodded, but otherwise they ate mostly in silence. Ronan stared at the middle of the table as if he were too tired to think, and she snuck surreptitious glances at him at intervals.

"I borrowed some clothes for you from my neighbor," she said when he had cleaned his plate of the second helping. He blinked, and she added, "So you can shower. Seems like you'd be more comfortable that way."

A few minutes later, he was in the bathroom trying to figure out the faucet while she finished cleaning the kitchen. The whole evening had a strangely domestic feel, as if it were practice for a future life, and she thought suddenly that she wouldn't mind a life with him.

She got out extra blankets and a pillow and arranged them on the couch, finishing just as the shower turned off. Several minutes later, he limped down the stairs.

She hadn't planned on him being so absurdly perfect. His damp hair fell in his face, and the dark circles under his eyes looked starker against his pallor. His shoulders were broader than Jerome's and his biceps larger, so that he filled out the shirt in a way that made her blush pink and look at the floor. Although he was tall, his legs weren't as long as Jerome's, so he'd rolled up the bottoms of the sweatpants, which would have looked utterly ridiculous on anyone else. On him, it merely looked charming. His bare feet stuck out, pale and slightly damp, as if he hadn't bothered to dry them. The grey mesh splint wrapped around his right foot nearly to his toes. The sleeve of the t-shirt didn't entirely conceal a ring of deep red punctures around his right bicep.

He held a bundle of clothes under his left arm, wrapped neatly in his enormous coat. "What would you like me to do with my dirty clothes?"

"I'll wash them." She took the clothes from him and put the entire bundle in the washer, hidden in a closet in the kitchen. "What about the coat? Does it need to be dry-cleaned or something?"

"I don't know what that means."

She examined the fabric. "Maybe? Probably? I'd hate to ruin it."

He shrugged and leaned against the wall. "It's already choked a kraken. I doubt your machine can do more damage to it."

He watched with interest as she measured detergent and started the machine. One of the turtledoves landed on his head and cooed cheerfully in greeting.

She glanced at the microwave clock. It was only eight, and normally she wouldn't go to bed yet. "I'm kind of tired. I was thinking about reading in bed for a while and going to bed early. Is that ok with you?"

"As you wish." He sighed. "I'm sorry, Charlotte. I didn't mean to intrude like this."

"It's fine." She smiled as brightly as she could, hoping it would cheer him, and was gratified to see a warm light in his golden eyes. "Maybe you can explain some things over breakfast?"

He hesitated, then said reluctantly, "As you wish."

"Goodnight, then."

He stood in the hallway and watched her ascend the stairs; she felt his gaze on her with mingled embarrassment and warmth. She locked the bedroom door behind herself, and the sound of the lock seemed startlingly loud. She flushed with embarrassment. Would he think she didn't trust him, even now? Strange as he was, she trusted him implicitly.

A moment later, she heard his cane thump softly as he made his way to the sofa, then a different thud, probably as he dropped it on the floor. Then there was silence.

Charlotte dove into her book and the world, along with worries about strange men with too many birds, fell away, and Faerie embraced her with its magic and wonder. The book was a retelling of Sleeping Beauty, and the characters were as enchanting as the story itself. Poly, the beauty, was amusingly frustrated with the absent-minded Luck, the enchanter who had freed her from the curse.

She turned the last page, aching for more, but thought she probably ought to go to sleep rather than start the next book. Her life had turned into a fairytale too, albeit without a lovely, neatly-wrapped-up ending that left everyone smiling.

Sleep drifted over her, soft and subtle, turning her worries into wonder and magic. She dreamed of an apartment filled with birds and of Ronan facing a dragon on an emerald hillside. She dreamed of Cormac, trim and elegant and terrifying, standing before a throne, with Ronan kneeling before him. Then the image floated away like mist evaporates in the sun, and she imagined flocks of birds wheeling and calling overhead.

They descended, turtledoves and ravens and swans and geese flocking together, their calls blending into a cacophony that swept over her.

She frowned and brushed a hand over her face, then snapped to wakefulness. Geese were honking downstairs.

On the Sixth Day of Christmas

Charlotte dressed hurriedly, scowling without realizing it. She burst out of the room and ran down the stairs to see Ronan staring contemplatively at six enormous geese who had settled in front of the book case.

"Good morning," she said, irritation making her voice sharper than she intended.

"Good morning." He stood to greet her, and his thoughtless courtesy made her ashamed of her irritation.

"Why are there more birds in my living room?" She winced at the plaintive tone in her voice. "I mean... what am I supposed to do with geese?"

Ronan huffed a soft, embarrassed laugh, and clenched his hand on his cane until his knuckles were white, and she knew that he was not nearly as amused as he wanted her to think. "I meant to give you something else. Something…" He looked down. "In Faerie, gifts are important. Your hospitality last night was both generous and charming, and the pleasure of your company was balm to my troubled heart. I meant to give you a gift of great value. In the human world, there are jewels and such that are of value, are there not?"

She nodded, and he darted a frustrated glance at the geese. "I intended to give you such a jewel, a bright red ruby that you could do with as you please. Wear it, sell it to buy something you prefer, give it as a gift to someone you love… it would have been yours." He cleared his throat. "But," his voice cracked, "but Cormac twisted my magic and gave you geese! No, he made *me* give you geese, and I don't know why, except that it entangles you more deeply in a spell that you've no reason to be tangled in."

"What spell?"

He opened his mouth, then closed it. "Do you want to know? Truly?" he said at last.

"Why do you not want to tell me?"

His jaw tensed and he turned away. He took a deep breath, and, still not looking at her, he said softly, "I fear you'll think it was some selfish plot on my part, when it was nothing of the sort. I've had little to do with it, other than… a sense of betrayal that my best friend, whom I've served honorably for many years, would so entrap you and blame me for it."

"Have you not seen him recently?"

Ronan's mouth twisted in a bitter smile. "Of course not. He goes where he pleases." Then he frowned, and said, "That was unfair of me. Cormac is Fae through and through; unpredictability is his nature and his pride. Yet

I thought I knew him; he's always been a faithful friend, inasmuch as a Fae can be faithful to anything."

"Are you human, then?"

"Yes, of course." He smiled in surprise.

"But that first night, you said, 'you hu-,' like you were about to say 'you humans.' I thought..."

She studied him with new eyes. One night of sleep in a warm house and a good dinner had revived him; the circles under his eyes were much faded, and his eyes had a gleam of wry humor in them as he watched her look him over.

At her prompting look, he said, "Most humans can't see in the dark, can they?" She shook her head, and he said, "Call it a gift of Faerie, then. One can't help but absorb a little magic over time."

Charlotte wondered what other magic he'd absorbed, and whether even he knew. His gaze on her face made her flush.

"Let's have breakfast," she said, partly to cover her embarrassment and partly because she really was hungry.

She cracked eggs into a bowl, measured oil and water, and poured in muffin mix, and then scrambled several eggs. Ronan watched with interest, and finally said, "How can I help?"

"Just get out plates and cups, I guess."

He looked in every cabinet before he found them.

"What's the spell that I'm stuck in?" she asked abruptly, then winced. "Sorry, that wasn't meant to sound accusatory."

He was silent for so long that she glanced up to meet his eyes, and he looked down. "If I tell you, it will change things, and I don't know if those changes will please you," he said at last. "It's your choice."

Her mouth felt suddenly dry. "All right. I think I'd still like to know."

He leaned against the wall, and guilt shot through her as she realized he'd grown paler, either at the thought of telling her, or perhaps merely at the pain of his ankle.

"The spell is a love spell, or at least an engagement spell," he said in a low voice. "Even Fae magic cannot compel true love, but it can… change… things, and people, not always for the better. This spell dictates that the 'true love' sends a recipient specific gifts of increasing value. The first is a partridge in a pear tree." She caught the flash of gold as he glanced at her surreptitiously. "The giver is the 'true love', but the spell doesn't specify whether the 'true love' is the lover or the loved one. Only that there is true love. At the culmination of the spell, there have been twelve increasingly outrageous gifts and… then what? I don't know what happens next."

Charlotte tried to still her racing thoughts. She admired him, felt affection for him, thought he was attractive… but was it love? He didn't seem particularly enamored with her. She spooned scrambled eggs onto the plates and pulled the muffins from the oven.

"And you've been trying to free me from it?" Did he dislike her or wish for her to be free? No, it would be more logical to assume that he merely wished to be free himself.

"Indeed." He carried the plates to the table while she poured milk into tumblers.

"Why is Cormac mixed up in it, then?"

Twelve Days of (Faerie) Christmas

He took a deep breath and bowed his head, and she imagined for an instant that he was weeping. No, perhaps he was only praying. When she looked up after her own prayer, he was looking at her with an expression she could not even begin to read. Evaluating her, considering his words and her reactions.

"Cormac changed my gifts," he said at last. "I don't know if the spell was his originally, but it is now. He could break it off, if he wanted to, but he hasn't. He would know when you received each new gift, because his magic is wrapped all through it; each gift reinforces the spell." A goose honked in the living room. Ronan closed his eyes in despair.

"Is it so bad, then?" she asked without thinking.

He made a strange noise of surprise and stared at her. "So bad? You should be free! You said it yourself—you had a good life until I showed up, and now your house is full of birds and your yard is full of monsters and I've invaded your living room! Not to mention causing trouble with your friends and associates."

She swallowed, feeling the sting of rejection that he hadn't actually voiced. "At least it's interesting," she said softly.

Ronan blinked, and then a strange, thoughtful smile flickered over his lips. "Although," he said in a low voice, "you don't seem as perturbed by the spell as I had anticipated. Is it not entirely horrifying, then?"

Charlotte hid her embarrassment in a cough. "I... well, I'm sure you'll be able to handle it. You're pretty competent, I think."

He blinked and tilted his head as he studied her. "I'm not sure if I should feel flattered by your overestimation of my abilities to unravel Fae spells, or distinctly wounded by your disinterest in me as a man." He watched her blush deepen, and that slight, dangerous smile danced over his lips again. But he said nothing else and looked away, giving her a chance to regain her equilibrium.

"So if you're human, how did you end up in Faerie?" she asked after several moments of silence.

"I was stolen," he said easily. At her look of surprise, he added, "Or perhaps I was sold to the faeries. Cormac never told me; I'm not sure if even he knows. Time is different in Faerie, of course; I don't know what year I was born, but it was long before all this—" he gestured gracefully at the townhouse "—was common."

"All this... what?" she asked cautiously.

"Electric lights, running water, gas stoves, that funny thing you call a phone but you rarely talk on... it's all new and strange."

She narrowed her eyes, trying to decide if he was teasing her, and he smiled, looking suddenly shy.

"Where were you born?" she asked.

"Somewhere in the Irish countryside. I was taken when I was quite young. I remember almost nothing of it." He shrugged as if trying to make light of it. "The world was green, and I remember playing by a stone wall once. Then it started to rain." He blinked and smiled, pushing away the memory. "That's all I remember. I've read books. It could have been in the 1200s for all I know, or the 1900s."

Charlotte stared at him. "Can't you just figure out from your age?"

He laughed. "Not at all. Faerie is *different*, you see. Nothing works the same way, not even time and aging.

So how old am I? I don't know. How old do I look?" He raised his eyebrows at her.

It was a surprisingly difficult question. He could have been anything from a well-muscled twenty to a fresh-faced, athletic forty-five. He watched her struggle with the question, and a teasing smile lifted his lips.

"Cormac is older than I am, though he doesn't look it. He was a young teen, or the Fae equivalent, when I arrived in Faerie, and he took me under his wing. We've been friends ever since." At this his voice tightened, but he said nothing else.

One of the geese honked proudly and waddled some feet away before settling down again.

"Oh, no. No no no," Charlotte muttered. "I don't want eggs on the carpet, please. Or messes!" She slid her chair back and started toward it.

The goose honked at her snidely and spread its wings, then settled down again with an irritated hiss.

"Oh!" She covered her mouth and stared at the pile of glittering jewels. "Oh my."

"What has it done?" Ronan said in a dangerous voice and hurried over. "Oh. That's all right, then."

"All right?" she squeaked.

"Sure. It's more or less what I meant to give you anyway, albeit with more birds and Fae magic." He bent to pick up the pile of jewels with both hands; Charlotte had a moment of fear that the motion was too precarious with weight only on one leg, but Ronan didn't seem unduly troubled by it. "Here." He poured the handful of rubies into her cupped hands.

"Is this real? Can it be real?" she whispered.

"They're real," he said encouragingly. "It's not much, of course, but perhaps it helps make up for a little of the trouble you've had on my account."

She let out a soft breath. "Do you really not know how much this is worth?"

"I did a little research on gem prices and average wages." She glanced at him, and he winked at her. "There's no point in a gift if you're stingy with it. I intended to be generous."

"This is more than generous."

He cleared his throat and flushed slightly. "Well, Cormac magnified my gift a little. But I did intend something much like this."

Another goose honked and waddled away, leaving a pile of enormous, perfectly white pearls.

Within minutes, the other four had also left piles of gemstones, including brilliant blue sapphires, sparkling green emeralds, green and pink tourmalines, and diamonds ranging from pink to white.

"What am I going to do with them?" Charlotte breathed. She flopped onto the couch, feeling as if the world were coming apart. "I can pay off my student loans! And my mortgage! But I'll get investigated by the FBI! They'll think I'm a criminal or something!" She buried her face in her hands.

Finally she looked up to see Ronan crestfallen. "It was meant to be a gift," he said. "Not a burden." He sagged and looked away. "Nothing is going right," he murmured.

The snow glinted pale blue and gold in the sunrise. Ronan stood at the window and looked out.

"May I have my clothes back?" he asked quietly.

"Oh! Let me dry them."

Ronan was still standing at the window when she returned.

"It takes about an hour to dry. But we have some time before I need to be at work."

Ronan smiled resignedly. "Thank you."

"I didn't mean to hurt your feelings," Charlotte said helplessly. "It's a beautiful gift, beyond generous! I just don't know what to do with it."

"Will it cause problems for you?"

"I'll figure something out." She stepped closer and looked out the window beside him. "Thank you."

He blinked and glanced down at her, as if the simple thanks had startled him in some way. "You're welcome."

An hour later, she pulled Ronan's warm clothes from the dryer and carried them to the bathroom as he limped up the stairs behind her. Several minutes later, he emerged looking surprisingly crisp. He'd splashed his hair with water and tried to tame it.

They rode to work in a comfortable silence. As Charlotte turned in to the tiny parking lot, Ronan said, "I must attend to several matters this afternoon. The colley birds followed us, and they will remain outside to provide you protection while I'm away."

Charlotte licked her lips. "Do you really think monsters will come here?"

"I hope not. But I would not have you unprotected."

He walked inside with her and strolled through the little office, looking through each open door. His gaze flicked around the lobby, and he stuck his head into her office for a moment before withdrawing.

"What are you doing?" she asked.

"It felt… different… today." He smiled reassuringly, green-gold eyes sparkling. "Never mind. Whatever it was, it's gone now."

Heather entered a moment later, stomping snow from her ballet flats and shaking flakes from her blue peacoat. "Oh, hat hair!" she grumbled. The fuzzy blue hat had tried, and failed, to flatten her bouncy auburn curls.

"You look gorgeous as always." Charlotte smiled. "Ronan, this is Heather. Heather, Ronan."

Ronan gave a polite half-bow. "It's a pleasure to meet you," he murmured, sounding ever-so-sophisticated.

"Likewise. So, you're Charlotte's mystery man?" Heather offered, with a mischievous glance at her friend.

Ronan blinked and glanced at Charlotte. "Well, um, I… perhaps?"

Charlotte's face flushed. "Definitely mysterious, and a man, so yes."

"I'll just go now, I think, Charlotte. Please stay in-doorsuntil I return this afternoon." Ronan waited until she nodded, then bowed and limped outside.

"You didn't tell me he was Dreamy McDreamer-son!" Heather whispered. "I mean, not that that changes what a horrible idea it is to let a stranger sleep on your couch, but you could have told me!"

"It's been an odd few days," Charlotte said help-lessly. "He's… he's helping with a problem I've found myself in the middle of, and I'm grateful, but it's also kind of confusing and scary and weird."

"Is *he* confusing and scary and weird?" Heather asked shrewdly.

"No, just confusing and weird." Charlotte hesitated, then added, "And dreamy and heroic."

"Heroic, huh?"

"It's a long story. Several long stories, in fact." Charlotte ran a hand through her hair and forced a smile. "How was Christmas?"

"Great! Everyone came, gifts, light display at the zoo; we did it all. My mom and I made orange chocolate truffles. I brought you and Jim each a box."

"Oooooh, DeFluiter family truffles are the best!" Charlotte grinned.

"They're really not that hard. I'll give you the recipe."

They dove into the papers. Heather answered the few phone calls and Charlotte concentrated on looking for the clues in the thousands of pages of documents. The day was mostly uneventful, although that afternoon she found a discrepancy in one of the papers, which she brought to Jim. He rubbed his jaw and nodded, looking cautiously pleased. "Thanks. This is good."

"Does this mean you can stop acting like a grouch?"

"I'll try, but no promises." He sighed and scrubbed his hands over his face. "Sorry."

Charlotte smiled gently. "Thanks." She hesitated, then asked, "Jim, what would happen if someone suddenly came into a sum of money?"

He gave her a sidelong look. "Like how much money? From where?"

"From… a friend, for example. Or imagine it was jewels."

"Gifts over a certain monetary value have to be declared to the IRS for tax purposes." Her eyes widened, and he added, "The giver pays the tax, not the recipient."

"Uh… hm." She chewed her lip. "Suppose the giver was unknown to the IRS. What then?"

"Like a drug dealer?" he asked with a shrewd look. "Or a man who claimed to be from Faerie?"

"Something like that."

"Well, yes, eventually the banks and the IRS would notice and investigate. Do the hypothetical jewels have any provenance?"

"Um… geese." Hysterical giggles threatened, and she said firmly, "Yep. Geese."

"Like the goose that laid the golden eggs?"

"Very like. Only sparklier."

Jim blinked. "Hm. An interesting problem to have. I'll have to think on it. I'm not a tax attorney, you know."

Charlotte was deeply engrossed in studying another batch of papers and didn't hear the door when Ronan entered the lobby just before 5:00.

Heather noticed his entrance. "Hi Ronan! You have a good day?"

"Yes, thank you," he said quietly.

He didn't look it. He looked cold and tired and annoyed.

"I'll be done in just a minute," Charlotte said. "Want anything while you wait? Coffee? Tea?"

"No, thank you." He sprawled bonelessly on the loveseat and stared at the ceiling.

Twelve Days of (Faerie) Christmas

"I'm headed out. Goodnight!" Heather called cheerily.

"Goodnight," everyone echoed.

Finishing that stack of paper, Charlotte put the last document aside and picked up her purse. "You ready?" she asked.

Ronan nodded and rose wordlessly, then nodded for her to lead the way out. At the door, he said, "You can leave me at the end of your street."

"Where are you sleeping tonight?"

Ronan looked down, clenching the head of his cane. "Here in the human world. I'll find someplace."

Charlotte sighed. "Is there something wrong with my couch?"

He let out a soft breath. "No, but…"

"It's 23 degrees and windy," she said quietly. "It would be awkward if I had to beg you to stay, don't you think?"

His lips quirked in a faint, grateful smile. "Well, I would never want to make you feel awkward. Thank you, Charlotte."

The way he said her name made her feel tingly and warm.

Another three inches of snow had fallen that day, leaving the city blanketed in pristine white. Though the roads were salted and plowed, the sidewalks were a jumble of snow and ice. Their parking lot was not plowed. Heather had shoveled the steps and a path to her car, shoveled out her car, and shoveled a space through the wall of snow and ice pushed up by the plow that was wide enough for her car to exit the parking lot.

"Phooey," muttered Charlotte.

"What?" Ronan asked.

"Don't worry, it won't take long. You should wait inside."

"For what?" he asked, apparently unfamiliar with the process of shoveling snow off from around a car.

Jim opened the door behind them. "Oh, snap," he said. "I meant to shovel you and Heather out but got stuck on that call. Give me a sec and I'll do it."

Ronan watched with interest as Jim retrieved a collapsible snow shovel from the back of his car. Charlotte did the same. The two of them began shoveling Charlotte's car out of the snow. "I can help," he said.

Jim glanced at him. "Don't worry about it. We'll be done in a minute."

Ronan limped down the stairs and made his way through the ankle-deep snow to Charlotte. "Please let me help."

"We're almost done! Look," she said.

"I'm sorry," he murmured.

Charlotte pushed the last bit of snow off the roof of the car and said, "See? We're done. Thanks, Jim." She put the shovel back in the trunk.

"No problem. See you tomorrow."

The drive home was silent. For dinner they shared a frozen pizza on the couch, watching the fire. Charlotte pulled her tiny ottoman over and insisted that Ronan put his foot on it.

"Does it actually feel better up, or did I just badger you until you gave in?"

His eyes glinted gold. "Yes."

She grinned. "Good. So what exactly do you do in Faerie?"

"I suppose you could say I work for the king. I'm one of a small force, led by Cormac, which seeks to prevent various dangerous Faerie creatures from entering the human world and causing havoc."

"Like kraken?"

"Among other things." He glanced at her from the corner of his eye. "I'll have you know that I'm generally rather good at my job, too. This," he gestured at his foot in irritation, "is, honestly, rather embarrassing."

"What, because you were attacked by a kraken and nearly drowned? I don't see what's to be embarrassed about."

He snorted and smiled reluctantly. "Well, if I'd planned to be in a love spell with you, I'd have devised a better introduction than being yanked into frigid water like a... a... I don't know. What sort of oblivious prey animals do you have in this part of the world? An unwary wildebeest attacked by a crocodile?"

Charlotte tried to stifle giggles. "You don't exactly remind me of a wildebeest."

"Why not? Because I don't have horns?" Ronan waggled his fingers above his head. "I can be rather hard-headed, though. Surely that counts for something."

"I have noticed that, yes," Charlotte said.

Ronan sighed contentedly. "I like your human food," he said. "What is this made of?"

"It's a flat bread made of wheat flour with garlic and olive oil. The red sauce is mostly tomato paste with herbs and spices, and the white on top is cheese." She glanced at him. "Have you never had pizza before?"

He shook his head. "No. Faerie food is... different. It's all quite marvelous and elaborate, of course, but intended for the Fae palate, not human." The skin at his eyes crinkled as he smiled. "Besides, my dining companion is lovely."

Charlotte blushed, and Ronan's smile deepened.

"Do you flatter all the girls?" she asked, mostly to cover her embarrassment.

He blinked. "What girls?"

"Um… it was mostly a joke."

He raised a hand and rubbed his face, pinched the bridge of his nose as if his head ached. "Your pardon, then. I misread your courtesy." He looked toward the pear tree again, then stood. He stacked her plate atop his, then carried them both to the dishwasher.

A knock on the door startled them both, and Ronan narrowed his eyes. "I'll get it."

"I can!" Charlotte jumped up, but Ronan beat her to the door. He flung it open, ready for anything.

Jerome smiled, dark eyes bright with curiosity. "Oh, hello. Nice shirt. Is Charlotte here?"

Ronan blinked and looked down at the borrowed lion shirt. He turned to Charlotte and, seeing her nod, stepped back from the door without a word.

"Oh, hello, Jerome! This is my friend Ronan. Ronan, this is Jerome. He and his wife Demetria live next door. He lent you those clothes."

Ronan's eyes widened. "I appreciate your generosity."

"No problem." Jerome's eyes raked over Ronan, evaluating his lean, muscular frame and shaggy curls, then slid to the many birds roosting quietly around the room. Charlotte had picked up the gemstones earlier and put them in a decorative basket on the mantel, but Jerome was easily tall enough to see inside. "What are those?"

"Um…" Charlotte stammered. "Um… they're… Ronan gave them to me. Sort of."

Twelve Days of (Faerie) Christmas

Jerome turned a skeptical eye toward Ronan but said only, "Demetria and I wanted to know if you want to come over for dinner Saturday night. We're making chicken satay and jasmine rice and a bunch of stuff. Demetria got the recipes from a Thai friend and she's all excited about experimenting. I hope you like being a guinea pig."

"Love it. That sounds delicious! What can I bring?"

The young man shrugged. "You want to make dessert?"

"You know me so well." Charlotte grinned. "Homemade cheesecakes with raspberry-chocolate sauce?"

Jerome laughed. "Who could turn that down?" He glanced at Ronan, who smiled courteously. "What did you do to your ankle?"

"I was just a little clumsy. Thank you for the use of your clothes."

Jerome studied him. "So where are you from?"

"Originally Ireland. But I haven't been there in many years."

"Why do you have so many birds?" Jerome asked Charlotte. "Starting an aviary?"

"Um... it's a long story." Charlotte felt her cheeks heating, even though she shouldn't have felt embarrassed. It wasn't even her doing!

"How long will you be here?" Jerome asked Ronan.

He glanced at Charlotte. "I... I don't know precisely."

"Maybe a week?" Charlotte guessed.

"All right. I'll tell Demetria you'll both be there. Hang on and I'll bring you some more clothes if you want."

Ronan's mouth opened wordlessly.

"That would be wonderful! Thank you," said Charlotte.

Jerome left and returned several minutes later with a stack of two tee shirts, two long-sleeved tee shirts, two sweaters, another pair of sweatpants, and a pair of track pants. "You can do laundry, so this should hold you 'til you get things sorted out."

Ronan took the stack of clothing with quiet wonder. "Thank you," he murmured. He limped to the couch and put the clothes in a neat stack at the end, then straightened, rather more pale than before.

As he left, Jerome stooped to whisper in Charlotte's ear. "Let me know if you need anything, Charlotte. We're right next door. Call any time, day or night."

"Thanks."

Charlotte locked the doors and checked that everything was off in the kitchen, and then stood in the doorway. "Goodnight."

"Goodnight, Charlotte."

ON THE SEVENTH DAY OF CHRISTMAS

The geese left glittering piles of gems in front of the bookshelves in the living room. When Charlotte came downstairs, she found Ronan sitting on the sofa with a goose in his lap, studying it eye to eye. A turtledove perched on his head.

"They really like you," Charlotte said.

Ronan smiled faintly, still studying the goose. "They're quite charming, when you get to know them."

"What are you looking for?"

He sighed and looked up. "A chink in the magic. Cormac's woven it so tightly I can't imagine a way to unravel it."

Charlotte toasted bagels for breakfast.

"What is this?" Ronan leaned forward, studying the bagel with interest. "It's like a bread, but round."

C. J. Brightley

"It is basically bread. It's called a bagel. I think they make the dough and then boil it in water for a minute before it's baked. It makes the outside crust have that chewy texture."

He watched her spread cream cheese over each half of her bagel, then did the same. "How fascinating. There are so many things I don't know," he murmured. Charlotte wasn't sure whether he intended for her to hear or not.

"Are you going to work with me again today?"

"If I may." He held her gaze steadily, and the green-gold of his eyes made her heart beat faster. "I must leave you for much of the day, but the turtledoves and colley birds will guard you while I am away. Also, the bracelet has protection in it."

She clenched her hands and then let the muscles relax, trying to decide if she was frightened or angry or grateful or merely confused. "How long are you staying, then?" she asked.

He pressed his lips together and looked down. "The end of the spell," he said at last. "Twelve days. This is day seven. After that..." He glanced up at her. "Well, we'll have to see." He smiled gently. "But if you're weary of me in your living room, I can find my own way well enough."

"I'm not kicking you out to sleep in the snow!" She frowned. "I just want to know what's going on."

"I'm trying to break the spell," he said. He took a bite of the bagel and chewed, his eyes closed in bliss. "Oh, I do like human food." He grinned at her, looking suddenly boyish. "Thank you, Charlotte."

She couldn't help smiling back.

Twelve Days of (Faerie) Christmas

Ronan walked through the office with her and checked each room before he left, saying he'd be back around lunch. Heather arrived as he was departing, and after she put her purse and lunchbox in her office, she slipped into Charlotte's office to whisper, "He's *incredibly* cute, Charlotte. Tell me the story of how you found him, again. I need instructions."

Charlotte laughed.

"No, really." Heather frowned at her. "What's the deal between you two? Are you dating? Friends? Acquaintances? Should I make eyes at him or not? Because if you're not interested, I might want to hint that I could be."

"Um…" The heat that flooded her face didn't help her play it cool. "Well, we're not dating or anything. But he's kind of busy right now…" She chewed her lip. He was kind, heroic, even-tempered, and sometimes even funny, and she *was* interested. Or at least she could be, if they could do something about the spell. "Well, I don't know."

Heather grinned delightedly. "Your face, Charlotte! Oh, you've got it bad, and I can't even blame you. You're adorable!" She flung her arms around Charlotte and giggled. "Don't worry, I'm not planning on poaching him or anything. Not that I could. He barely glanced at me."

"I don't have it bad!" Charlotte protested helplessly.

Heather pulled back, still giggling. "Oh, yes you do!" She sighed happily. "Now, what can I do to help?"

Charlotte leaned back and groaned. She'd been staring at papers for hours, and everything seemed to check out. She couldn't find any other discrepancies to support Jim's client's case. Only one more box remained.

She rubbed her eyes and considered another cup of coffee.

The door dinged softly as Ronan entered the waiting area, brushing snow from his dark hair. He smiled when he saw her, and the warmth in his gaze made her heart jump.

"Are you hungry?" she asked. "I need to get out of the office for a minute before my eyes cross."

"All right." He waited while she put on her coat and retrieved her purse from under her desk.

"You can stay if you don't want to walk," she offered belatedly. "I can just go."

Ronan frowned. "Do I look that pathetic?"

Charlotte asked Heather and Jim if she wanted them to pick up lunch for them. Jim stared at her blankly for a solid ten seconds with unfocused eyes, and she repeated her question. "Do you want something from Breadbowl? I'm going to pick up lunch." Jim looked… a little rough, if she were honest. "Jim, did you go home last night?" she asked.

He blinked. "Lunch?" He scrubbed his hands over his face and shook his head. "No, I took a nap here. I found most of what I need for Perry's case but I need to put it together…" His attention drifted back to the computer screen.

"Lunch!" Charlotte prompted. "From Breadbowl. Is a turkey bacon sandwich all right?"

He glanced at her again. "Um. Yes. Sure. Are you going?"

Charlotte tried not to smile. "Yes. I'll be back in a few minutes."

Their shoes crunched on salt and ice as they walked two blocks to Breadbowl at a leisurely, careful place. After Charlotte ordered, they stood off to the side to wait.

"Any progress?" she asked.

"No." Ronan's jaw tightened, and he looked down. "I'm sorry, Charlotte."

"It's not your fault."

"But nothing's happened today, yet. Right?"

He smiled faintly. "Indeed. Your optimism is heart-warming, though I fear I will not measure up to your expectations."

Charlotte bit her lip but said nothing else.

The sandwich shop hummed with activity. After several moments, Ronan said quietly, "Thank you for bringing me here. It's fascinating."

She glanced up at him and nearly grinned to see his eyes flicking over each part of the little restaurant with interest. He watched the process of making each sandwich, each order of soup spooned into a bread bowl and topped with a circular plug of bread. He watched the patrons enjoying their meals, some alone, others in small groups huddled around little bistro tables. A selection of house-made salad dressings and just-roasted coffee beans lined one wall; he read each label curiously.

"Have you never eaten at a sandwich shop before?"

"No." He glanced down at her. "I've rarely been in the human world for more than a few hours at a time.

C. J. Brightley

Aside from your hospitality, I haven't eaten human food since I was a young child."

She blinked. "What about when you *have* been in the human world for more than a few hours? How long was it? Didn't you eat anything?"

He shrugged easily. "A couple of days. I just waited." At her disgruntled look, he added disarmingly, "I was busy!"

Charlotte frowned thoughtfully and stretched to whisper in his ear. He leaned down obligingly; his dark curls tickled her cheek. "Do you like the human world?"

He let out a soft, agonized breath. "I love it with every fiber of my being. But I can't stay."

"Because of the spell?"

"I belong to Cormac's father. He'd never let me go." He swallowed. "Faerie is a wondrous place, full of magic and beauty I cannot comprehend, much less describe. There is much to love there. But this is a home I've always longed for, knowing it could never be mine." He huffed a soft, mirthless laugh. "Not that I know how to be human anyway."

"You're doing a fine job of being human," Charlotte said, so softly she wasn't sure whether she intended him to hear or not.

He did, and he whispered, "Thank you."

A young man behind the counter called "48." Charlotte, much to Ronan's consternation, insisted on carrying the bag of sandwiches. "No, see? It's not even heavy! You need to have your hands free anyway."

Ronan finally gave in, looking disgruntled, and they set off back toward the office.

"So what do you do all day when you're not in the office with me?" she asked.

"Just... work. Go here and there and deal with magic."

"Do you walk?" She imagined him limping all over the city, fighting magical monsters on every street corner.

He shrugged. "Well, sometimes I take shortcuts." At her curious glance, he smiled. "Like when I was meeting Cormac. There was a doorway to Faerie in that wood, if you know how to open it. I know where they are, or where they will be for a short period of time, and I can open them. Cormac can make a doorway wherever and whenever he wants, but... well, he's Cormac and I'm not."

"So the doorway wasn't always there, but you knew it would be there?"

"Exactly."

The wind whipped across the Potomac, flicking up flakes of snow and cutting through Charlotte's coat. She shivered. "Do you like the work?"

"Love it. Well, most of the time." He frowned. "Well, some of the time. I find purpose in it, and it lets me visit your world. Do you like your work?"

She smiled. "I find purpose in it, even if I don't love every minute of it. And I like Jim and Heather."

Ronan's eyes narrowed, and he stared over the water. "He's done it again," he muttered.

"Done what?" Charlotte asked.

He gestured wordlessly toward the Potomac, where seven magnificent swans swam toward them.

"Swans?" asked Charlotte incredulously.

"Swans a-swimming," grumbled Ronan. "Cormac's magic is wrapped around them like silver netting, all glittery and elegant and smug, like only a Fae can be."

The swans reached the bank and clambered up one after another, heading straight for Ronan and Charlotte. They were much bigger than Charlotte had expected, and a thread of fear curled through her belly. She fought the urge to run.

Ronan glared at the enormous birds as they waddled closer. "Get on with you!" he muttered. "You're only making things worse."

One of the swans opened its beak and hissed at him menacingly. He gave it a withering look of scorn. "Silence, you overgrown son of a buzzard. You take your six siblings right back to Cormac and tell him to stop meddling in things that don't concern him."

Three other swans hissed at him and waddled ever nearer, their large black eyes fixed on Charlotte.

She gave a little *eep* of surprise when one of them pecked at her hand, and quick as lightning, Ronan swatted the bird between the eyes with the back of one finger before it touched her. "Leave her alone!" he barked.

The swans, now arranged in a circle around her, all flapped their wings in unison.

She felt an odd sensation of falling, and a cloud of sparkles flickered in her eyes, as if she'd just looked at a strobe light.

As if in a dream, she saw a spacious study, lined with tall bookshelves and expansive windows. The bookshelves stretched to the ceiling some five stories above her head, but no ladders offered access. Cormac leaned far back in a chair, booted feet crossed atop one corner of an elegant wooden desk; in another corner, well away from his feet, sat an inkwell and a quill pen. He gestured carelessly with one hand and a book flew from one of the top shelves in a graceful arc to land on the desk. He pulled glittering magic from the air and wove it into an intricate cats-cradle netting. His quicksilver eyes followed the netting as he rapidly wove it from a few strands to a densely knotted blanket draped over his hands.

Cormac glanced up to meet her gaze and smiled delightedly. "Oh, hello," he murmured.

Fear flooded her veins, and she would have screamed, but before she could inhale, he tossed the sparkling net over her head.

There was a thump.

She was sitting in the snow.

Ronan knelt in front of her, looking rather pale.

"Are you all right?" he said urgently. "You just went down without warning. Are you dizzy?"

Charlotte swallowed, feeling a faint, pleasant buzz at the back of her brain, and said carefully, "I'm fine. I feel… fine, I guess. I feel sparkly."

"Oh, that's not good," Ronan breathed.

She realized, with a warm thrill, that he'd steadied her with one hand on her shoulder. Maybe that was why she felt sparkly. "What's not good? Where are the swans?"

"Gone." He shifted, and his face went white as a sheet.

She rose easily, finding that the buzz and warmth and sparkles did not make her unsteady in the least. If anything, she felt more energetic and alive than she had five minutes ago. What a strange dream! It slipped away even as she tried to remember it. "Are you all right?" she asked.

"I'm fine," he said, and it was such an obvious lie that she would have laughed at him, if she hadn't been so worried. "Nevertheless, I'd be grateful if you would allow me a moment."

When he'd pushed the pain down to a manageable level, he stood, wobbling a little.

"What exactly happened just then with the swans?" she asked.

"Cormac happened," Ronan said bitterly. "The threads weave ever tighter."

A gust of icy wind whipped at their faces, and Ronan swayed, his knuckles white on the head of his cane.

"Let's go inside," she said.

He stayed long enough to eat his sandwich in the tiny conference room with Charlotte and Heather. Ashen and silent, he listened while the young ladies chatted about Heather's family's Christmas adventures and summer plans.

When he was finished, he tossed the sandwich wrapper in the trash, stood, and murmured, "Stay inside until I return, please, Charlotte." He waited until she nodded before he left.

Heather studied her. "What's up with the 'stay inside' business?"

"He's just... protective."

Heather made a skeptical face. "Stalker type? He doesn't seem creepy enough."

"No. It's... no, he's just being careful. I'm fine with it for now."

Her friend studied her face curiously. "You think there's a good reason for him to be like that?"

Charlotte hesitated, then nodded. "Yes. Honestly, I appreciate it. I don't think the danger will last much longer, anyway."

Twelve Days of (Faerie) Christmas

She breathed a quick, heartfelt prayer for his safety.

An hour later, Charlotte found what they'd all been looking for. She confirmed it, then hurried back to Jim's office. "Ta da!" she sang. "I found it. Look!" She stuck the paper under his nose. "Look? See there? This money should be here and it's not."

Jim took a swig of coffee and took the papers, following her explanation. He yawned. "Yep, ok. And this one here…" He ran his finger down a column of numbers on another sheet. "Ha! We got him."

He stretched his arms up, and Charlotte heard his back crack."Right then. What time is it? 1:30." He yawned again and rubbed his jaw tiredly. "All right, I'll finish this motion, file it, and then I'm done for the day."

"Do you need me to come in tomorrow?"

He sighed. "Trade you next Friday for it? I have a hearing first thing Monday morning and I need that brief. Can you finish it tomorrow?"

"Sure thing."

He left at 4:45, just as Charlotte and Heather had expected, because he was a perfectionist. Perfectionism took precedence over an early bedtime. But the motion was filed, and everyone breathed a sigh of relief.

Ronan returned just as Jim was leaving. He nodded a courteous greeting to Heather and leaned against the wall while Charlotte got her purse.

"Are you all right?" Heather asked.

He blinked, startled. "Me?"

"Yes, you." Heather smiled, amused. "You look like you had a rough day."

He brushed hand self-consciously over his hair, already disheveled and covered by fat snowflakes. "Sorry," he mumbled.

The two ladies and Ronan walked together to the parking lot.

Once they were in the car, Charlotte asked, "How was the rest of your day?"

Ronan was silent for so long that she glanced at him, wondering if he planned to answer. Finally he said, "Busy."

"How's your ankle?"

She heard the smile in his voice when he answered, "Fine. It's healing. It just takes time."

At home, they microwaved leftovers for dinner. Afterwards, Charlotte suggested, "Let's just read for a while. What do you like to read?"

"Everything." Ronan smiled. "Most of what I've read is old, though. I'd like to read one of your favorites, if I may."

She handed him the book she'd just finished and picked up the sequel for herself. Within moments, she was fully engrossed in the story of Annabelle, Peter, and Blackfoot. With the fire crackling softly, snow falling outside, a good book, and good company, she relaxed into the story.

Hours later, Charlotte stretched and looked around. The hens had already gone to sleep in a corner; the fire had made the hearth too warm for their comfort. The geese had congregated beneath her little Christmas tree, their heads folded beneath their wings. A stray ruby on the carpet glinted in the firelight.

Twelve Days of (Faerie) Christmas

The turtledoves had settled on the back of the sofa by Ronan's head. He'd dozed off with his fingers splayed across page 168.

"Goodnight," she said softly.

He blinked and looked at her blankly for a moment, then down at the book. "Goodnight, Charlotte. Thank you."

"For what?"

"For... for a..." He glanced around helplessly. "For a warm room and a fire and a book and a dinner and a hot shower and good conversation." A faint pink tinged his cheeks. "I mean before I fell asleep." His flush deepened. "I'm sorry. I didn't mean to be awkward."

She bit back a giggle and said, "You're welcome, Ronan."

A look of startled pleasure flashed across his face, and he smiled so sweetly that she couldn't breathe for a moment.

"What did I say?" she whispered.

"That's the first time you've called me by name, except for when you introduced me to your friend." His eyes sparked warm green-gold. "I like how you say it."

If he smiled like that again, she'd be in love.

ON THE EIGHTH DAY OF CHRISTMAS

Friday morning was bizarrely uneventful. They enjoyed a quiet breakfast and Charlotte packed sandwiches and spinach salads topped by cranberries and walnuts while Ronan studied the pear tree again, lost in thought. They drove to work through a light snowfall that served more to freshen the city than to clog the streets.

"I'll be back this afternoon," Ronan murmured to her. "Remain inside, if you please."

"What about lunch?" Charlotte asked.

"You packed something."

Charlotte frowned. "I mean *your* lunch. I packed you a sandwich too."

He blinked. "Why?"

"Um, because people generally prefer not to be hungry?" She shrugged self-consciously. "I couldn't very well pack a lunch for myself and nothing for you. I mean, I guess I could but it wouldn't be very nice." Her cheeks heated. "Anyway, I packed you a lunch. You should take it with you."

He chuckled, his green-gold gaze warm on her face. "You're very kind."

She pulled out his sandwich bag, plastic container of salad, and a fork. "Here." She handed them to him, and his fingers lingered on hers, warm and strong, before he stuffed the food into a coat pocket.

"Thank you."

As Charlotte was finishing her salad, there was a *whoop!* from Jim's office, and then the sound of a chair hitting the wall. Heather and Charlotte looked at each other in confusion.

Another sound, like shuffling feet. Heather followed Charlotte to Jim's door. Charlotte opened it hesitantly, and they both peeked inside.

Jim was dancing a jig with his hands in the air and a grin on his face. When he saw them, he froze, eyes wide, and slowly lowered his arms.

"Sorry," he said stiffly. "Ignore me, please."

Charlotte blinked. "Uh, no. No, I will not. Care to share the good news?"

Jim's face flushed. "Just… got a dinner date next week. As one does, you know."

Heather smiled gently. "Is that why you've been so grumpy? Nerves?"

"I've been out of the dating game nearly as long as you've been alive, you whippersnappers." Jim glared at them in mock outrage. "It's not easy, you know." He flopped down in his chair. "I'd ask you what restaurants are good, but I'm not cool enough for the places you probably go."

Charlotte laughed. "I'm not cool, Jim. I mostly cook at home."

"Oh." He frowned, then asked plaintively, "Then how am I supposed to look suave? You're no help!" He ran his hands over his salt-and-pepper hair, then said, "We never did a company Christmas dinner. You have plans tonight?" He glanced at them both.

"Not really," Heather said. "Tonight works for me."

"Um…"

Jim gave her a shrewd look. "Bring a plus one, then."

She smiled gratefully. "All right."

The door dinged merrily, announcing Ronan's entrance.

"Hello! What did you do all day?" Charlotte asked with a smile.

"Oh, not much. Just… work." Ronan smiled back, his eyes lingering on her face.

"You look cold." The pink flush on his pale cheeks was unexpectedly adorable.

"Maybe a bit. I won't mind warming up while you finish."

He sat in the waiting area so quietly that Charlotte, focused on the contract Jim had asked her to draft, nearly forgot he was there.

Twelve Days of (Faerie) Christmas

Jim knocked on the doorframe and said, "Hey, time to go."

Charlotte grabbed her purse and hurried out to the lobby, where Ronan had fallen asleep, his head braced on his right fist and hair fallen over his eyes. He held an old book encased in plastic wrap in his lap, his left hand covering the title. His cane leaned against his right leg.

Heather raised her eyebrows questioningly at Charlotte and leaned closer to whisper, "Is he just bored or what? Also, it's completely unfair for someone to look so good while they're sleeping."

Jim pretended not to hear and opened the front door. "You coming?" he said more loudly than necessary.

"Sorry." Ronan blinked awake and thrust the book into a coat pocket, then ran his hand over his face and through his hair; Charlotte wondered whether he knew it was charmingly disheveled or whether he was oblivious.

He smiled and politely waited while the others preceded him out the door.

When Charlotte followed Jim and Heather down the street, he looked momentarily confused but followed along. "We're going to dinner," Charlotte said. "You're invited too."

"Oh," he said carefully. "Where?"

"I don't know. I think Jim mentioned Bertucci's." She glanced at him and added, "It's Italian."

"Oh."

Jim stopped and turned, looking guilt-stricken. "It's about three blocks. Can you walk that far?"

"Yes." Ronan looked vaguely affronted at the question.

They walked in silence for several moments, Jim and Heather just ahead of them. The streets were full of tourists enjoying the historic area as well as corporate workers walking from their offices above the retail fronts to their cars in nearby garages. They walked three blocks, then turned and walked another half block before entering the restaurant. Charlotte glanced at Ronan's face several times, trying to gauge how much pain he was in, but it was hard to tell in the shifting illumination of storefronts and streetlights.

Jim muttered, half to himself and half to Heather, "I feel like a jerk. I didn't even think, and there's no parking."

Ronan's lips quirked in a half-smile, but he said nothing.

At last they reached Bertucci's, and, much to Charlotte's surprise, there was no wait for a table. They followed a trim waiter through the main room to one of the quiet tables in the back, where he placed menus on the table and informed them of the wine selection and specials. He left them to consider their choices.

Ronan murmured in Charlotte's ear, "I have no idea what we're doing." The warmth of his breath tickled her ear.

She whispered back, "Choose something that sounds tasty and then tell the waiter when he comes back."

"I have no idea what's tasty."

"Get the ravioli. It's pretty safe."

He gave her an odd look. "Are the other dishes unsafe?"

Jim chuckled. "Are you always so literal?"

"Not always," Ronan said. "I'm a little out of my element here."

Heather's eyes sparkled. "Where are you from, Ronan? How did you meet Charlotte?" She put her menu aside and smiled at them.

The waiter returned that moment with their drinks and asked for their orders, so Ronan effortlessly avoided the question for several more minutes.

"Well? Tell us about yourself, then," Heather prompted.

"There's not much to say. I met Charlotte by chance a few days before Christmas and managed to misplace my coat, which she kindly returned to me." He smiled guilelessly, as if that had answered the question.

Jim snorted. "And somehow you're now escorting her to work every day? Is that part of returning her coat?"

"My work, much to my regret, has inadvertently put Charlotte in some small amount of danger. I'm here to ensure her safety while the matter is resolved."

The older man nodded. "And now we get to the heart of the matter. What exactly do you do?"

"I'm not at liberty to discuss it."

"Are you a spy?"

"What?" Ronan blinked.

"A *spy*. A foreign intelligence officer." Jim's eyes narrowed. "We don't deal with anything you'd want. None of my cases have international import. But this is the outskirts of Washington DC, and when someone comes around with sketchy explanations for their weird behavior and far too much money, I can't help but think they're covering up something very real, very logical, and very dangerous."

Ronan sat back with a faint, amused smile. "You think I work for a foreign government? Well, suppose I did. What would you do?"

"What do you think I'd do?"

Charlotte put her head in her hands. "Please stop!" she whispered. "He's not a spy, Jim. I promise."

"Give me a reason to believe you," Jim said to Ronan.

"I'd rather avoid that, actually. Most of the events proving my words over the last few days have been unpleasant or inconvenient for Charlotte." He flattened his hands on the table and studied them thoughtfully. "Yet I understand your skepticism. You might say that I work for a family that prefers to remain discreet. Charlotte was present at, and, to our mutual dismay, involved in an operation several days ago. Thus, my duties now require that I protect Charlotte for a period of time until everything is settled."

Jim sighed. "That was one of the more uninformative answers I've ever heard."

The waiter arrived with a basket of house-made donuts and cinnamon butter, along with a platter of drinks. Jim pulled out his phone and began to dial surreptitiously.

"Please don't," Ronan said quietly. "I've already had one run-in with the police this week." When Jim continued dialing, Ronan reached across the table and slipped the phone out of his hand so quickly that Jim couldn't stop him. At nearly the same moment, a shadow skittered down the wall and across the table toward Charlotte. Ronan grabbed it with his other hand, deposited Jim's phone on the seat between Charlotte and himself, and then repositioned the creature to avoid its pincers.

"It's not really a matter for the police anyway," he added. He pressed the head of the creature to the table with his right hand and flattened its long, segmented body to the table with his other hand and forearm.

The creature was a dark, cloudy gray that seemed to suck in the light around it, leaving it more shadow than substance. The segments of its body reminded her of a giant centipede. But its legs were longer and hairier than any centipede she'd ever seen, not to mention that the creature itself was eighteen inches long. The head, too, looked vaguely like that of a centipede, but for the three-inch pincers that protruded from the bottom of its head and the long, stalk-like eyes that waved furiously.

Jim stared at it, wide-eyed and silent; without noticing, he was edging himself between Heather and the creature, pushing her out of the booth into the aisle. Heather made a little squeak of fear.

Ronan slid his left hand up a little farther to control the creature's head while still using his left forearm to mash the creature's body to the table, preventing it from knocking over their water glasses. This freed his right hand, which he used to pick up a fork and stab the creature.

It disintegrated into a cloud of glitter and a faint scent of ozone. He blew it at gently, and the cloud disappeared.

Ronan inspected the fork, wiped it carefully on a napkin, and set it back its place.

"You're still going to use that fork?" Charlotte asked in bemusement.

Ronan shrugged. "Faerie bits don't stay in the human world. It's perfectly clean." He glanced up at Jim and Heather. "It's gone."

"What was that?" Heather whispered.

"Just a little nuisance, not particularly dangerous." Ronan handed Jim's phone back. "I apologize for my rudeness. I can't fault you for thinking me a little strange, not knowing about Faerie and its many dangers, but I give you my word I pose no threat to Charlotte. Neither am I a spy for a human government."

A waiter cleared his throat. "Um... what was that?" His voice cracked.

"Nothing to worry about," said Ronan.

Seeing the waiter's panic, Charlotte added brightly, "Just a little magic!"

The waiter blinked and nodded, skeptical but willing to be mollified. "Right. Sure. Like for a magic show."

"Exactly."

The waiter delivered their food and retreated.

"Why'd it disappear?" Jim asked suddenly. "Why the glitter and sparkles?"

"It's a creature of Faerie. Stainless steel contains iron, you know." Ronan smiled delightedly. "What a glorious surprise when I discovered that little fact! It makes my work here much easier." He held up a fork and admired it. "Lovely little weaponry, this silverware. I tried to take a piece back with me once but it didn't work." He shrugged philosophically. "Probably for the best, though. If things could go back and forth that easily, we'd have all sorts of problems. Not to mention the political repercussions."

"The glitter?"

Ronan shrugged. "Faerie is magic. I think the sparkles are the friction as the magic slides back through the barrier to Faerie. But it could be just the magic burning up, like the sparks that fly up from a campfire."

"Why is Charlotte in danger?"

"I'd rather not discuss it. It's complicated."

"I'm a lawyer. I can handle complicated."

Charlotte smiled. "It's a different kind of complicated. I'd rather not talk about it right now, either."

"Are you scared?" Heather asked.

Charlotte considered the question. "I'm not, actually. Ronan's pretty confidence-inspiring." She glanced at him just in time to see a flicker of surprise and pleasure in his eyes.

"I'll endeavor not to disappoint you," he said softly.

Dinner was surprisingly relaxed, and they laughed with Heather over her recounting of her family's various escapades over the holiday. Jim, his concerns about Ronan at least somewhat assuaged, asked leading questions of Heather and Charlotte to keep the conversation going when it might have become awkward.

When the waiter brought the check, Jim handed him a credit card and he took it away again.

"Thanks, Jim," said Charlotte and Heather.

"What are we thanking him for?" Ronan murmured in Charlotte's ear.

"For dinner." Technically it was a company dinner, and he'd probably used the company credit card, but as the sole owner of the company, it was still his money."

"Thank you," said Ronan seriously.

Jim nodded. "Sure thing. Welcome. Merry Christmas."

Ronan, remembering something, said, "I have gifts!" He smiled to himself as he began digging in the pockets of his coat. "Here." He handed the plastic-wrapped book to Jim and a small wooden box to Heather.

The lawyer frowned as he examined the book. "What's this?" He carefully opened the plastic wrap on one end and let the book slide into his hand. *A Tale of Two Cities*. This is old. Where did you get this?"

Ronan smiled secretively. "Ah, but that would spoil the fun, wouldn't it?"

"1859! This is a first printing!" Jim sucked in a breath as he examined the book. "This must have cost a *fortune*. I can't take this. I've seen one in a museum in worse condition." He looked up at Ronan, baffled. "Why did you get me this?"

"You have a set of Dickens on your office shelves, but it's missing this one. This isn't the book academics like best, but it was always my favorite of his works." Ronan smiled easily. "Don't feel too beholden; I had several copies, so it is a pleasure to give one to someone who will appreciate it."

"Several first print editions?" Jim sat back, his mouth hanging open. "I can't even imagine."

"Well, there were more of them on the market when I obtained them." Ronan turned to Heather. "I apologize; I didn't have as much of an idea what you might like. So I opted for something useful." He nodded that she should open the box.

The wooden lid was inlaid with elegant whorls and leaves, all polished to a subtle shine. Heather flipped it open to reveal a neatly folded handkerchief. She pulled it out and unfolded it, frowning faintly.

"A handkerchief?" she asked in confusion. It was quite an elegant handkerchief, with her initials monogrammed in one corner.

"It cleans quite well," Ronan offered.

Heather looked confused and slightly disappointed, though she tried to conceal it. "Thank you."

Ronan hesitated, then said hopefully, "Try it?"

"It's all right. Thanks."

He licked his lips and then nodded, looking rather deflated. "Perhaps it's not that exciting after all."

Charlotte suspected there was more to the handkerchief than was apparent. "What does it do?"

"It cleans," he said again. "Like this." He held out his hand for the handkerchief, which Heather handed him bemusedly. He wiped the handkerchief all over his plate, thoroughly dirtying the handkerchief and leaving the plate spotless. Then he folded the handkerchief up into a neat square and unfolded it again, revealing pristine white cloth. "See? It cleans anything."

Jim blinked and leaned forward, studying the cloth. "But where does the stuff go? I mean… does it go anywhere or does it just vaporize or what?"

"It obeys all the laws of physics. Well, mostly. Conservation of energy and matter and all that. It just… well, I don't know exactly where it goes. Elsewhere. It's magic." Ronan frowned. "I would ask Cormac, but…" He shrugged, trying to look careless but mostly looking disgruntled. "Anyway, it isn't much, but I thought it might come in handy."

Heather took the handkerchief, still looking confused. "Thank you." She wiped it against the side of her glass experimentally. The fabric soaked up the condensation, leaving the glass completely dry. Then she wiped the handkerchief over a tiny spot of tomato sauce that had splattered onto the white tablecloth. The spot vanished.

"It's magic," she said softly.

Ronan nodded. "Indeed."

Charlotte thought suddenly of Ronan's dirty clothes in which he'd apparently slept for several days, and asked, "Don't you have one of your own?"

"Not anymore."

Heather stopped and stared at him. "Was this one yours? You don't have to give it to me!"

Ronan blinked and hesitated. "Well, not exactly. I lost mine to a griffin a few weeks ago, and that was going to be my new one, but I thought it would make a good gift. They're a bit fiddly to make, especially for me since I'm not Fae and can't see the magic very well, so I couldn't very well make two of them in one day, not while attending to my other responsibilities." He smiled warmly. "So it's yours!"

Charlotte murmured, "Why don't they get birds?"

"That's what I want to know," Ronan replied, not bothering to conceal his irritation.

Heather made a questioning face at Charlotte, who said, "I was just asking him why you didn't get birds. I got lots of birds."

"Geese?" Jim asked innocently.

"Six of them. Two turtledoves, a partridge in a pear tree, four ravens, and three French hens."

"They're colley birds," Ronan murmured. "They don't like the term raven. Last time I called them ravens they screamed 'Nevermore' at me."

Jim guffawed, then stopped, red-faced. "You're not kidding?"

Ronan looked baffled. "Not at all. They're quite opinionated about it."

They walked back to the office at a leisurely pace. The air was icy but still, with barely a breeze off the water. A few snowflakes drifted gently from the sky, lending the picturesque historic streets a magical glow.

"What's that?" Heather asked. She leaned forward to examine something in a window box.

Ronan's eyes glinted gold, and he growled, "Cormac's doing." He looked around, but it was clear that he did not expect to actually see the Fae prince.

"Who's Cormac?" Jim asked.

A muscle in Ronan's jaw tightened, but he said only, "A friend."

"What is it?" Charlotte edged closer and knelt beside Heather, who was staring in awe at eight tiny fairy maidens hiding under the leaves of a snow-covered begonia. "Ronan, what are they?"

"Eight maids a-milking," he said cryptically. "I'd hoped… never mind."

"But you didn't give me a gift! How could Cormac twist your gift if you didn't give me one?" Charlotte frowned.

"Should I have?" he murmured. "Perhaps…"

"No! I'm not saying you should have! I just want to understand."

He knelt beside her, studying the little fairies. They rubbed the underside of a begonia leaf, producing a thin greenish liquid on their minuscule hands, which they licked with evident relish.

"They're not milking anything," Charlotte said, with a vague sense of injustice. "How can they be maids a-milking if they're not milking? They're juicing it or something!"

Ronan gave a startled laugh and glanced at her out of the corner of his eye. "It's close enough for the spell, unfortunately."

"Still, you didn't give me a gift. Doesn't Cormac need a gift to work with?"

Ronan studied her face. "Did you want a gift?" he asked, with gravity that surprised her.

"No! I just want to know how it works."

"The spell used my action to protect you during dinner as a gift." Ronan nodded politely to the little fairies, who waved to him cheerfully, and then stood.

"Well, that makes it hard to not give me gifts, doesn't it?" Charlotte muttered. "Since I doubt you're planning to leave me to my own devices against Faerie monsters."

"Indeed."

❀n the ℕinth 𝔇ay of ℭhristmas

reams faded like mist in the golden warmth of sunlight. A thin layer of fresh snow made even the early light brilliant. Charlotte stretched luxuriously in bed, letting the light wash over her. She snuggled into her pillow and closed her eyes again.

A faint, rhythmic sound caught her attention, but she resolutely ignored it for several minutes. The sound grew louder and more insistent.

Finally she left her bed, pulled on her bathrobe, and marched downstairs.

"What is going on?" she cried over the noise.

Ronan stood in the center of a ring of diminutive drummers, nostrils flared and fists clenched as if he were trying valiantly not to box their ears. "You're finished!"

he roared over the deafening drums. "You've done it! Now go home!"

The drummers looked up at him with wide eyes but continued without a pause.

Ronan grabbed one of them by the arm and the waistband and flung him bodily toward Charlotte's wall mirror. Charlotte shrieked, the sound lost beneath the cacophony, expecting injury to both the drummer and the mirror and appalled at Ronan's violence. The drummer sailed happily through the mirror and disappeared. The room seemed infinitesimally quieter.

Tall and implacable, Ronan disposed of each drummer the same way. The drummers did not seem to fear this fate, which reassured Charlotte.

When there was only one drummer remaining, he stopped playing and looked up at Ronan. "Apologies, your lordship. Orders. You understand, don't you?"

Ronan sighed and nodded. "Sure, Angus. I know. Get on with you."

Angus bowed to him, then caught sight of Charlotte and bowed much more elaborately to her. "Well met, fair lady." Then he leaped through the mirror, leaving only the reflection of Charlotte's living room.

"What was that all about?"

Ronan slumped. "The ninth day. Nine drummers drumming. The web tightening." He glanced at her, then sank to the sofa, his face buried in his hands.

Glittering like a dragon's hoard in the sunlight, emeralds, tourmalines, and diamonds lay scattered across her hearth. Pearls and sapphires gleamed in front of her bookshelves, and rubies shone beneath the window. "Will the geese leave me gems every morning?" she asked. "I keep thinking it's all a dream."

Twelve Days of (Faerie) Christmas

Ronan leaned back with a groan. "Yes, they should. That magic isn't time-bound like the trap we're in." His golden eyes flicked between the birds, each in their favorite spot. The geese looked back at him smugly.

"Do you have any plans today? Any place you have to be?" Charlotte asked.

"No." He rubbed his hands over his face and then looked up at her. "Oh. Cheesecakes. I don't know what those are."

"A deliciously decadent dessert that we will make. But first I have to go to the grocery store."

She wished, for an instant, that he would stay home. Not because his company was unwelcome—it was disconcerting how much she enjoyed his quiet presence—but because grocery shopping was never fun, and it was probably even less enjoyable with a much-abused broken ankle.

Seeing her expression, he said quietly, "I beg your pardon. You must be tired of me by now, but I really must accompany you. You're glittery and bright with magic, and I'm slower than usual; I couldn't forgive myself if something happened and I were too far away to help you."

"I was thinking of your ankle, actually."

He blinked. "It's fine. See?" He stood, bracing himself only a little on the arm of the sofa as he did so.

"If you say so," she said doubtfully.

Even the grocery store was interesting to Ronan. "Have you never been in a grocery store before?" she asked, when she caught him surveying the fruit and vegetable section with delighted surprise.

"Never."

Charlotte stocked up her usual items, adding cream cheese, sour cream, heavy cream, extra eggs, frozen raspberries, and graham crackers.

Back at home, she showed Ronan how to read the recipe, then laid out all the ingredients and turned the oven on.

"May I taste them?" he asked.

He'd never tasted any of the ingredients! So she gave him a taste of each ingredient in turn, pausing at the vanilla extract. "This is pretty strong. It's better once it's mixed with stuff."

He gazed at her expectantly. "I've eaten some pretty strong things before. I'll try it."

"Sure."

To his credit, he didn't make a horrified face at the strong flavor of the pure vanilla extract. Instead, his brows lowered and he looked thoughtful. "Interesting," he murmured at last.

She showed him how to crush the graham crackers and mix the crumbs with sugar and melted butter. She showed him how to use the mixer to mix the cream cheese, cream, and sour cream together with sugar and vanilla.

While the cheesecake baked, she narrated making her raspberry fudge sauce.

"This is a great deal of effort," he said from where he stood leaning against the pantry door. "Do you enjoy it?"

She smiled. "Yes, I do. I wouldn't want to go to this much effort every day, of course, but it's fun to bring something fancy to a dinner party." She stirred the raspberries in a pot on the stove. His gaze on her face made her cheeks heat.

"Thank you for sharing it with me," he said quietly.

While the cheesecake cooled, they sat in the living room in front of the fire and read. It was quiet, peaceful, and exactly what Charlotte needed after a productive morning.

She looked up from her book to see Ronan dozing with his head braced on his fist. One of the turtledoves had nestled against his leg, content as a kitten, and the other sat beside his head on the back of the sofa, looking out the window with bright black eyes. His dark curls fell over his eyes as if he'd arranged them that way, though she was quite sure he hadn't. His borrowed tee shirt showed the lean muscle of his chest and arms and the slow, steady rhythm of his breathing. It really was not fair at all that someone should look so disconcertingly perfect while sleeping!

The hens muttered to themselves in amusement. *Vous venez de remarquer qu'il est joli, n'est-ce pas? Ne t'inquiète pas, il ne le sait pas non plus.*[11]

"What?" she whispered to them.

Qu'allez-vous faire à ce sujet? C'est un homme bon, Charlotte, et aussi brillant d'espoir que vous le voudriez. Tu ne penses pas que tu pourrais l'aimer?[12]

The only words she'd understood were *brilliant* and her own name. Were they telling her Ronan was brilliant? Why?

Ronan sighed and rubbed his eyes blearily. "Stop meddling, you nosy little biddies."

---

[11] *You just noticed that he's pretty, didn't you? Don't worry, he doesn't know either.*

[12] *What are you going to do about it? He's a good man, Charlotte, and as bright with hope as you could wish. Don't you think you could love him?*

They cackled merrily. *Nous aidons juste! Tu es si lent, Ronan. Nous devons être sûrs qu'elle est prête le moment venu.*[13]

"Ready for what?" He gave them a narrow look.

Tic, tic, bang![14] They stared at him expectantly, and he stared back as if trying to read their enigmatic little hen expressions. The silence drew out for long moments, and then, as one, the hens turned to hide their heads beneath their wings.

"Oh, so that's it?" he growled, in a voice that seemed as if he were both genuinely irritated and playing it up for effect. "You're going to ignore me now because you're too chicken to tell me the truth?"

Charlotte covered her mouth to hide her smile.

"I thought we were friends," he muttered, mostly to himself but with one eye on the hens. They shrank smaller, as if ashamed of themselves, but did not raise their heads. He sighed and rolled his eyes.

At 5:30 they stepped out into a winter wonderland. Snow drifted downward in fat flakes, already six inches deep on the grass. Charlotte's patio was shoveled, as were the three steps, the sidewalk and every other little patio on that side of the street. The other side was nearly finished. Charlotte stopped and waited as the figure at the end shoveled the last patio, hoisted the shovel over his shoulder, and started back toward them.

"That was really nice, Jerome. Thank you!" called Charlotte. "You didn't have to shovel everyone's steps."

Jerome shrugged and grinned. In the twilight, his white teeth stood out against his dark skin. "Yeah, but I

---

[13] *We're just helping! You're so slow, Ronan. We must be sure she's ready when the time comes.*

[14] *Tick, tock, bang!*

didn't go to the gym this morning, and I was going to do ours and Mrs. Donahue's anyway, so I figured why not?" He ushered them inside and took off his parka and hat. Demetria called out a greeting from the kitchen.

Charlotte brought the cheesecake and pot of sauce into the kitchen, where she offered to help Demetria with any last minute preparation.

"Oh, it's all done! The rice just needs a few more minutes, and the chicken satay is in the oven. I'm broiling it rather than grilling, but I think it'll work. Jerome wants to play a board game my brother got him for his birthday. Go out and listen to the rules. I'll be there in a minute." The young woman smiled, her dark eyes bright with good humor.

The game was already set up, carefully arranged so that they could play even while they ate. A centerpiece of white candles stood at the end of the table, out of the way of their game. Jerome explained the rules while Demetria finished the food. They filled their plates (not without some argument about who ought to go first) and sat down. Jerome prayed for the meal.

While they played, they chatted about work and family. Jerome and Demetria asked Ronan polite questions, and he answered everything without actually revealing much about himself at all.

After an enjoyable evening that included a second round of dessert, Charlotte and Ronan bid their hosts goodnight and walked next door.

"Goodnight, Ronan."

"Goodnight, Charlotte."

On the Tenth Day of Christmas

C harlotte woke to the smell of bacon and cinnamon rolls, and lay staring at the shadowed ceiling for several minutes, wondering at the strangeness of her life. She dressed blearily and wandered downstairs to find Ronan in the kitchen looking rather flustered.

"Do you need help?"

"I'm fine," he said. "Though modern American kitchens are more intimidating than I'd realized." He found a potholder and pulled the muffins out of the oven. "Yet even I can learn when sufficiently motivated."

"You're that hungry?" Charlotte teased.

He shot her a golden look. "It seemed like a gift even a Fae would struggle to twist." A plaintive wail came from the front yard, and Ronan's eyes narrowed.

"It seems I was overly optimistic." He turned off the stove and limped grimly to the door.

He jerked it open with a stifled grunt of pain, and the sound of bagpipes washed over Charlotte with astonishing volume.

Ten Fae wearing green and gold livery marched triumphantly around the cherry tree, playing with gusto.

"What are you doing?" Ronan called in a commanding voice.

The bagpipers glanced at him but continued playing, albeit with a slightly intimidated air.

Neighbors up and down the street began opening doors and looking out windows.

"Don't blame them." Cormac had been leaning against the tree trunk in the center of the marching pipers, and now he stepped forward with a slight bow. "A lovely gift for a lovely lady, Ronan." The pipers stepped around him, continuing to play as he drew closer.

Ronan's nostrils flared. "She is indeed lovely, my prince, but you must stop."

An icy wind gusted, blowing snow in Cormac's face and sticking in his hair, where it disappeared against the white-blond fluff. He waved a hand and the pipers disappeared, their sound fading into a glittering tension. "No, I mustn't," he said softly.

Ronan, with some effort, made his way down the steps to the snow-covered grass.

The Fae prince bowed mockingly. "Until tomorrow, Charlotte, Ronan."

Ronan limped forward. "Cormac, as you love me, free her! You've no right to entrap her like this!"

"I don't?" Cormac's eyes glittered. "Might I remind you of the authority I hold over your very life?"

"I haven't forgotten it. Yet I thought I thought we were friends! Please, Cormac!"

"Absolutely not."

Ronan's fist hit Cormac's face with a sickening crack. The Fae's head snapped back, and he stumbled backward.

There was an instant of awful silence.

Cormac straightened slowly. His nose and mouth bled freely down his chin, a shocking red against his unearthly pallor. Drops of blood dotted the snow like discarded rubies. Lightning flashed over his hands and up his forearms, and his eyes flickered with white-hot power.

"That was unwise," he said in a low voice.

"I know." Ronan's voice shook. "Free her before you kill me, if we've ever been friends."

Cormac's gaze flicked toward Charlotte and back to Ronan. "No." His voice was flat and hard. Then he smiled coldly, and the blood in his teeth made him look like a nightmare. "Two days, Ronan. Use them well."

Then he ripped a hole in the fabric of the world and stepped through.

Ronan doubled over, burying his scream of rage in his hands.

Across the street, Mrs. Donahue covered her mouth with both hands. She hurried inside, and Charlotte imagined she would call the police. Aggravated Assault. Battery. What else? Loitering? Trespassing? Attempted murder?

Ronan made his way back inside, white-faced and grim. Behind him, drops of Cormac's blood stood out crimson against the snow.

Charlotte stepped aside as Ronan limped past her, then closed the door carefully.

"I hope breakfast is edible," he muttered. "I pray I've done one small thing right."

Charlotte fixed their plates while he leaned against the wall with his arms crossed over his chest. Brows furrowed, he looked from the partridge in the pear tree, to the turtledoves, to the French hens, to the colley birds outside, to the geese, their piles of jewels, and every other gift.

"What happens at the end?" Charlotte asked.

"I don't know."

Terror fluttered at the edge of her mind, but she forced it back. "Then why is he doing this? I don't understand."

"Neither do I." Ronan's voice was rough with emotion.

"Will it hurt you?"

"I neither know nor care! The magic is wrapped around you so tightly I wonder that you do not feel it. I cannot think what grievance he would have against you, but it's pulling so hard."

Charlotte hesitated, trying to determine if she felt different in any way. "I... I'm just worried," she confessed. "He seemed so dangerous."

Ronan's huff of bitter laughter startled her. "Indeed. He's the most dangerous creature in either of our worlds."

"He didn't kill you, though." Mingled fear and relief made her voice shake.

"Not yet." He dropped his head into his hands. "I don't know what to do," he whispered.

"Well, let's eat breakfast, at least." She nudged him toward the table. "I have to be at church soon."

He nodded and ate quickly; Charlotte wondered whether he actually tasted any of the food. She ran upstairs to brush her teeth.

"Have you ever been to church before?" she asked, feeling oddly nervous about it.

"A few times," he said quietly. "It hasn't been... possible... as often as I'd like." He gave her a sidelong glance. "Thank you for taking me."

He listened intently to the worship music and even more intently to the sermon. After the service, he murmured polite greetings when Charlotte introduced him to her many friends of all ages. One, white-haired and elegant in a pink tailored suit, embraced Charlotte and said, "It's good to see you with a nice young man, Charlotte! Tell me about yourself, Ronan, is it?"

Ronan smiled charmingly. "Oh, there's not much to tell. You have a lovely church. Thank you for welcoming me."

Another friend whispered interested questions in Charlotte's ear. "Where did you meet him?"

"At the Harbor." While chatting with her friends, Charlotte shot surreptitious looks at Ronan periodically. He was surprisingly good at deflecting probing questions without drawing attention to his evasiveness. Brandon, a friend's husband, questioned him about his work, accepting Ronan's vague answers as an indication of a connection with one of the many intelligence agencies in the area.

They ate lunch with a group of single church members at a fun little bistro with a salad bar and soft serve ice cream, which fascinated Ronan.

"What is it?" he whispered to Charlotte.

"Ice cream. A dessert. You can put those toppings on it if you want."

Ronan studied the buckets of chocolate chips, diced nuts, gummy animals, cherries, and other toppings with a baffled eye. "Why? What are they for?"

One of the college students nearby chuckled. "I don't know either. It's best plain."

Ronan enjoyed the meal without revealing anything about himself other than delight with the food and pleasant conversation. No one but Ronan noticed that Charlotte paid for both of them; he glanced across at her with a puzzled, then grateful look.

On the short drive home, he said quietly, "Charlotte, I owe you so much. I can't imagine how I would ever repay you, if I had time."

Charlotte glanced at him out of the corner of her eye, wondering whether he was entirely serious. "I think saving me from numerous magical monsters is a good start."

He frowned thoughtfully. "Not really."

They spent the afternoon taking down Charlotte's Christmas tree and other decorations. Ronan seemed quieter and more pensive than usual.

"Is something bothering you?" Charlotte finally asked.

He smiled, the kindness in his eyes nearly hiding the grief. "I'm thinking about the spell, wondering if there is any crack I might widen or any missed stitch in the weaving I might pull upon to loosen it and free you." He swallowed and looked down. "Alas, I have failed."

"Well, you still have two days, don't you?" She tried to keep her voice steady.

Something in his eyes flickered, some emotion quickly hidden, and he murmured, "Your faith in me is both misplaced and valued beyond measure."

ON THE ELEVENTH DAY OF CHRISTMAS

O n Monday, Charlotte woke at her alarm, stared at the ceiling, and pondered the wonders the day would hold. She dressed and wandered downstairs to make a quick breakfast.

At office, Ronan walked through the office, checking for magical dangers before he bid her farewell. Work was utterly uneventful, and Charlotte welcomed the quiet of the day. Jim was out of the office for the hearing, and she heard nothing from him until 4:00, when he texted *Hearing went well. Good work.*

At 4:30, Charlotte wondered whether Ronan had been injured in one of his adventures. At 4:45, she wished he had a cell phone. At 4:55, Heather asked her, "Where's Ronan?"

"Out doing… stuff."

Heather glanced at the front door. "Dangerous stuff?"

"Probably." Charlotte bit her lip. "But I'm sure he's fine."

Three minutes later, the door dinged and Ronan limped inside, brushing snow from his hair.

"Busy day?" Heather asked brightly.

He blinked. "You could say that, yes."

Charlotte took in his unusually rumpled appearance and asked, "Anything exciting happen?"

"Nothing worth mentioning." He smiled innocently and leaned against the doorframe. "How was your day?"

"Quiet."

"Good," he said.

After dinner, Charlotte showed Ronan how to make brownies and put them in the oven, then ran upstairs to shower. "Sit and relax for a minute," she urged.

"Thank you." He settled on the sofa with his foot up on the ottoman.

Twenty minutes later, she skipped back downstairs wearing fuzzy flannel pajamas, expecting to find Ronan still on the sofa with his foot up, perhaps even asleep.

He was still on the sofa, but now he was studying one of the pears.

"What do you think?" he murmured to one of the hens. It answered him in French, and his eyes narrowed. "Hm. I'm not sure."

"What did she say?" Charlotte asked.

He glanced up at her. "Oh, she doesn't know anything about the magic." The hen pecked his wrist sharply, and he winced. "Ouch! Fine, I'll tell her. She says you're bright with magic, all wrapped up like a fly in a cobweb." He frowned. "I don't agree, though. If it were that sort of spell, you'd feel it by now. How do you feel?"

"Fine." But when he caught her eye, such an odd, fluttery sort of feeling came over her that she added quietly, "Just a little strange, I suppose."

"How so?" Ronan twisted to fix his green-gold eyes on her face, and the sudden intensity of his gaze made her flush with embarrassment.

"Not bad! Just... strange."

Strange in that there was a *man* on her couch, and every time she looked at him she had a harder time looking away. She fled to the kitchen and pulled the brownies from the oven, then stood there alone for several minutes, trying to decipher a flood of unfamiliar feelings.

Eventually she heard Ronan stand and the quiet thump of his cane as he limped through the living room. She cut two brownies and turned to the cabinet for dessert plates, avoiding his gaze.

"Have I offended you in some way?" he asked quietly.

She swallowed, looking at the floor. "No, I don't think so. I'm just... you've frightened me, I think."

He sucked in a quick breath and stepped back. "Forgive me."

She choked out a laugh. "No, not you, but the things you say. I don't *feel* trapped, not like you say, but you're so sure of it that I doubt myself. I wonder whether my feelings are real or if they're just a side effect of the magic."

Her heartbeat thudded in her ears.

"Feelings?" His question was so gentle, so soft, that it slipped past what little control she'd had on her emotions.

"Exactly! Feelings! It's not fair at all that you come tromping into my life all gallant and heroic and put upon, and not expect a girl to have feelings! It was utterly and completely predictable, I suppose, but I still don't know what to do about it. Am I supposed to love you, or is that just the spell? I don't feel like it's the spell, but how would I know?" She wiped at her eyes angrily. "And I hate that I cry when I'm embarrassed! It's totally unhelpful!"

Ronan covered his quick chuckle with an elegant cough. "I beg your pardon, then. I'll endeavor to not notice any tears, much as it pains me to do so." Then he sighed. "Charlotte, I… I'm not particularly well-versed in human expressions of regard." He caught one of her hands in his and bowed over it, dark hair falling over his face. The kiss was featherlight against her knuckles, so soft she almost thought she'd imagined it. "Please believe me when I say that your presence in this time is a pleasure I cannot describe. I regret the burden I have been, but I treasure every moment with you."

Charlotte sniffled, then carefully pulled away, wishing she could throw herself into his arms. "Let's have some brownies," she whispered.

"As you wish," he murmured, and if there was a depth of grief in his voice that made her heart twist inside her, she ignored it. She didn't know what it meant, nor how she should respond, and her own grief and confusion felt like an immensity that might swallow her at any moment.

She put the plates on the table and sat down, only to realize that Ronan had stepped away and crossed the living room to stand at the window.

"What's wrong?" she said, trying to keep her voice from shaking.

Ronan craned his neck, looking up the street in both directions. Then he turned and limped to the front door with startling speed. He flung it open and hurried out, pulling it closed behind him. "Stay inside!"

She peeked out the door anyway.

Without warning, an enormous creature swooped at Ronan from the sky, and Charlotte screamed.

Each scale was the size of her hand, the color of an oil slick or an iridescent beetle. At the sound of her voice, its enormous head whipped toward her.

Orange eyes gleamed.

It struck like a cobra.

She fell backwards with a terrified cry and pulled her legs behind the door just as the creature's jaw's snapped shut. Ronan slid his sword into the creature's side. It whipped toward him, engulfing his head and torso in its huge mouth. It began to writhe, wrapping thick coils of snakelike body around his body even as it drew its head upward. It meant to rip him to pieces.

A diminutive fairy danced through the air, silver robes twinkling and sparkling, and skittered down the creature's neck with a faint bell-like cry. Ten others followed. Shedding sparkles, they danced and spun like snowflakes around the beast's head.

Panic flooded her veins. Charlotte grabbed the largest knife from the block in her kitchen and ran toward the creature. She would have screamed, if she'd felt braver, but instead she was silent and terrified.

When she was two steps from the wyvern, it turned its orange eyes toward her, and she nearly froze.

But Ronan needed her, and she raised the knife above the huge scaled coil before her.

It burst into a cloud of glitter and sparkles.

The fairies danced away, laughing.

Ronan fell ten feet and landed with a grunt of pain, softening the blow with a roll that spared his injured ankle the worst of the impact. He curled onto his side.

The glitter blew away, leaving only the faint scent of ozone and remembered terror. Charlotte lowered the knife and stepped cautiously toward Ronan. "Are you all right?"

He groaned.

That was worrying. He'd always said he was fine before. She hurried closer and knelt beside him, setting the knife down in the snow a safe distance away.

"Should I call an ambulance?" Her voice shook.

"No," he croaked. "Are you all right?"

"I'm fine," she said. "But I'm not sure you are. What's broken?"

"Nothing." But he curled into himself and closed his eyes. "Just give me a moment, please," he breathed.

Frowning with worry, she sat back and looked him over carefully. No blood caught her eye, and the mesh splint around his ankle seemed to be undamaged. His hair was damp with melted snow and some clear viscous slime. Something had pressed against his neck and shoulder hard enough to leave a bright red mark.

"That was entirely unpleasant," he rasped finally. He groaned as he sat up, and she leaned forward to help him. "Don't touch me. I'm slimy."

She smiled. "You look like you need the help."

"I'd rather look dashingly unperturbed by that experience," he muttered. "But I'll settle for mostly in one piece."

"Well, you did look rather heroic," she offered.

"Did I? I mostly felt…" He frowned and let out a pained breath, folding his arms across his chest and curling inward. "Oh, that was unpleasant," he groaned.

"You said that already," Charlotte said.

"It bears repeating," he said firmly. "Wyverns are awful."

"Where did it come from? Why was it here?"

Ronan looked grimly at his sword and the cane sheath several feet away. "Cormac's magic draws them like bees to nectar. He's magic, through and through, and everything that ever considered opposing him will see you as a tasty little morsel." He swallowed and pressed his arms over his chest again, wincing. "I'm surprised there haven't been more attacks." He studied her with narrowed eyes.

After several minutes, they made their way inside, which took a worryingly long time. Ronan grew white-faced and silent, and Charlotte felt worry fluttering in her chest like a caged turtledove.

"Go upstairs and take a hot shower. You'll feel better."

"You're right." He sagged against the wall. "I will."

The hens clucked at him from the hearth, and the turtledoves flew agitated circles in the living room.

She thought he was going to faint, but after a moment he pushed himself upright and limped upstairs. He leaned against the vanity while Charlotte brought a new set of borrowed clothes and a fresh towel, then started the water for him.

She busied herself preparing the couch for him while she waited. The image of the wyvern's eyes on her, of its mouth engulfing Ronan's body, replayed in her mind. The cobra-like speed of its strike. The subtle silver at the edge of each beetle-bright scale. The glittering orange eyes.

Ronan took quite a long time upstairs, and she tried to believe it was because he was enjoying the shower, not because he'd lost consciousness or something equally worrisome.

Finally the water stopped, and she breathed a sigh of relief.

He made his way downstairs, leaving heavily on both his cane and the banister. "Thank you, Charlotte. I feel much recovered."

She studied him with narrowed eyes. "You look it," she said in a dry voice.

"The comfort of your sofa is not to be underestimated as a restorative, either," he said. One of the turtledoves landed on his head and scrabbled in his wet hair, eliciting a wince. "Have you still not eaten a pear?" he asked suddenly.

"No."

"Would you, please?" He sank to the couch and picked up the pear he'd been examining before the wyvern attack. Charlotte noticed, with scarcely a moment of surprise, that the tree again bore three perfectly ripe pears, having immediately regrown the one Ronan

TWELVE DAYS OF (FAERIE) CHRISTMAS

had picked. The turtledove on his head hopped to the back of the couch and folded its head under one wing sleepily.

"Why?"

He offered her the pear. "I want to see what the magic does when you eat it." He saw her hesitation. "Are you frightened?"

"Perhaps a little." She laughed at herself. "I'm sorry. That must seem rather silly to you at this point."

He opened his mouth, then pressed his lips together, reconsidering his words. Finally he said, "All right." He put the pear aside and smiled kindly.

Charlotte felt a rush of gratitude, and then, "Oh! The brownies!" She jumped up and brought the plates over.

At the first bite, Ronan's eyes widened. He chewed meditatively, swallowed, and said, "That was quite possibly the most delicious thing I have ever had the pleasure of tasting."

She laughed, and he said seriously, "I wasn't joking."

The hens flapped their wings and muttered to each other in satisfied tones. *C'est tellement évident! Comment ne le voit-elle pas?*[15]

A muscle in Ronan's jaw tightened, and he murmured, "Gardez vos becs en dehors de cela. Ce n'est pas ton affaire."[16]

"What?" Charlotte asked.

"I told them to mind their own business," he said stiffly. "They're... meddling." The turtledove behind him pecked him in the back of the head. "Ouch! Stop it!" he muttered. "They *are* meddling little biddies."

---

[15] *It's so obvious! How does she not see it?*
[16] *Keep your beaks out of this. It's none of your business.*

The partridge protested sleepily from the pear tree, and he rolled his eyes tolerantly.

They finished their brownies in a comfortable silence.

Charlotte took the plates back to the kitchen and washed them, trying to decipher her feelings.

She called "Goodnight" softly, and received no answer.

ON THE TWELFTH DAY OF CHRISTMAS

When her alarm buzzed quietly on the nightstand, Charlotte turned it off and stared at the ceiling, wondering at the silence downstairs. Faint blue-gold light peeked in the windows and gilded the edge of her comforter. She dressed quietly and slipped downstairs, wondering if Ronan had left.

The living room was dark. The hens watched her quietly, three little crimson heads turning in unison to follow her as she looked toward Ronan's spot on the sofa.

He was still asleep. He was too tall to fully stretch out on the sofa; he lay curled on his side with one arm under the pillow, long legs bent with his feet against the sofa arm. His long eyelashes looked nearly black against his pale skin. Under the blanket, his other arm seemed to be curled protectively around his stomach.

Charlotte hesitated, feeling a disconcerting urge to kiss his cheek, and then shook herself. She stepped into the kitchen and began making pancakes and scrambled eggs.

Soon the pancakes were cooked and the eggs were scrambled. Golden morning light streamed through the windows across the living room carpet.

Charlotte knelt in front of him. "Breakfast is ready."

His eyelashes fluttered, and he sighed softly but did not wake.

"Ronan," she whispered. She touched his shoulder gently, and he blinked awake, his eyes wide and startled.

"What's wrong?" He sat up, paled, and wrapped his left arm around his stomach while his right hand found the head of his cane. No, he was already drawing his sword.

"Breakfast is ready," she said softly.

He swallowed and glanced around the room, then relaxed. "Oh. Sorry." He leaned back with a long, pained breath.

"Are you all right?" Charlotte asked.

"Just sore," he muttered. "No major damage. Just… squished and sore." He stared at the ceiling. "Anyway, there's not long now."

He followed her to the table. "This looks delicious. Thank you, Charlotte."

"You're welcome."

They prayed silently.

"You really ought to tell me what's going on," Charlotte said. "There's a love spell, yes, but you said there's an end to it. Right?"

"It ends at midnight." He studied his scrambled eggs as if he'd never seen them before. Perhaps they were a new food for him, but he'd eaten them several times in the last week, so she knew he was avoiding her gaze.

"What happens at the end, then?"

"I don't know exactly." He sighed. "It's ticking like a clock… or a bomb… and it ends at midnight. But I don't know what it *does*."

"What does it look like, then? How can you tell anything about it? How do you know it ends at midnight?"

"I feel it pulling on me, and I feel the endpoint approaching, looming ever closer. All I can tell is that there will be a bang."

"A bang? That sounds ominous."

"Indeed." He glanced at her. "You understand my concern."

"What do you think happens? I mean, what sort of bang?"

The turtledove on his head cooed softly, and he frowned. "A very, very *big* one. Big enough to break things. Or people." He looked across the room at the pear tree and the various birds in their favored places. "Cormac's magic is wrapped around them, binding them to each other and to you. And to me. He has a luminous, silvery, glittery sort of magic, bright as sunlight but cool and subtle as water, so even when you're looking right at it, you can't really be sure you understand it all."

"What's your magic like?" Charlotte asked.

157

He snorted. "Mine? Mine's a sort of walnut color, staid and boring. What you see is what you get with me." He glanced at her, as if wondering if she were disappointed.

"Can you undo Cormac's magic and stop the bang?"

"It would take a miracle and a half." Ronan smiled ruefully. "No, I can't think of anything I can do to stop him now." He took a deep breath and let it out slowly, studying her across the table. No, he wasn't studying *her*; he was studying the magic she could not see, his green-gold eyes bright and focused.

"I don't think it will harm you," he said finally. "I didn't see it at first, because the rest of it is so very strong and bright, but beneath all the spiky bits and the parts that slip through me, pulling on the magic binding me, there's a formidable layer of protection around you." His focus softened, and he met her eyes for a moment. "He means you no harm, and indeed has taken great care that even the Unseelie creatures eager to taste his magic would have a very unpleasant surprise if they dared touch you." He leaned forward, studying the magic again. "I wish I had seen that earlier. That wyvern should be grateful it met the end of my sword before it touched you. There wouldn't have even been sparkles left if it had touched you."

Charlotte smiled tentatively. "So he's good? Cormac, I mean?"

Ronan snorted. "He's Fae. He's unpredictable and deceptive and dangerous. But yes, if ever a Fae were 'good', Cormac is. Yet this spell... I see protection, but also the... whatever it is... ticking slowly down to midnight, a bang big enough to turn this whole city to ash. And you and I are in the center of it."

Twelve Days of (Faerie) Christmas

The turtledove scrabbled on his head as if it wanted to make a nest in his hair. He winced and removed it, folded its wings down gently, and held it on the table. It glared at him balefully and cooed. "Hush, I'm trying to concentrate," he muttered. His green-gold eyes flicked over its body, to the pear tree with the sleepy partridge, and then to the French hens, and back to Charlotte. Then he sighed and let the bird go. It flew to the top of the bookshelf and gave him a dirty look.

"The spell tightens with every word between us," he said softly. "I'd suggest staying silent, but there's not much point in that now."

Charlotte swallowed. "If I pretend I'm not afraid, will it help?"

Ronan raised his eyebrows. "I would expect no less of you. Your courage and kindness throughout this ordeal have been a very great help indeed." He smiled shyly. "I regret that a spell has brought us together; such circumstances are hardly ideal. But if I have to be in a love spell with someone, I can think of no one I would prefer over you."

She smiled, then frowned, then laughed at herself and blushed. "I could say the same. Thank you, Ronan." She put her hand on his, feeling simultaneously bold and tentative. He froze, green-gold eyes wide with surprise. A faint flush pinked his cheeks. Then he folded his hand around hers, warm and strong.

He looked down at their hands and narrowed his eyes. "You've grown very spiky indeed," he murmured.

"Spiky?" she whispered. "Is that bad?"

His eyes flicked over her face and body with an almost clinical interest, glinting a deeper gold than usual. He squeezed her hand, let it go, and stood to examine her from every angle. Charlotte sat still, feeling her face heat yet again.

"What exactly are you looking at?" she asked, wishing her voice didn't sound quite so tremulous.

Catching sight of himself in the hallway mirror, he stood stock-still, his gaze flicking from her to her reflection and back again. He rubbed his sternum absently and shifted, examining her reflection from a new angle.

"Well, that's reassuring," he said at last, with an air of quiet satisfaction.

"What is?"

He sat down again and smiled. "You'll be all right. The bang won't hurt you at all." He swallowed and glanced away for an instant, then looked back to meet her eyes seriously. "There is no harm in it for you, Charlotte." He hesitated, then reached for her hand tentatively. When she put her hand in his, he held it between his larger hands as if it were something precious, his long fingers loosely cradling hers. After a moment, he bowed his head solemnly and kissed her knuckles, his lips warm and bright as candlelight on her skin.

"What about you?" she whispered.

He shook his curls out of his face and gave a careless half-shrug. "Cormac has his reasons, I'm sure," he murmured.

"That's not much of an answer."

Ronan pressed his lips together and looked down at their entwined fingers. "You'll be fine," he said again.

She sucked in a breath. "And you won't. You're saying you won't, aren't you?"

He half-shrugged again, and smiled faintly, still looking at their hands. "I can't imagine how I'd survive." He rubbed his thumb gently over her knuckles, exploring the contours of each delicate bone. "I imagine I'm being asked to make a grand sacrifice on behalf of all humanity." He glanced up, a teasing smile dancing around his lips. "Only Cormac hasn't asked me, because of some complicated magical reason. He's Fae; not knowing what he's doing is hardly unusual. I've spent most of my life trying to keep up with his whims." His smile softened, and he sighed. Charlotte had the disquieting feeling that he felt more affection than resentment toward his friend.

"Aren't you angry?" she whispered.

He swallowed and said quietly, "Angry as death. I only wish he'd tell me what he's doing. I'd die for him, and he for me, or so I thought. But," he smiled, cheeks pale and eyes bright, "if this is what I must do, then it is what I must do. It won't be a pointless sacrifice." His smile sharpened a little, a dangerous glint in his eye. "Cormac is many things, but he's never careless with his magic. This spell is far too complex to be an accident. Every little nuance of it, every gossamer-thin thread of glittery silver magic binding us together, binding the birds and the gems and the golden rings, everything else... he has a reason."

"You're very brave."

The words startled him, and he let out a soft huff of laughter. "Not at all." But then his gaze met hers, and he murmured, "Though the words are a gift I cherish. I would have you think the best of me."

Tears filled her eyes. She looked down and brushed at her eyes surreptitiously, knowing he saw but grateful that he said nothing. "I'm going to take the day off," she whispered.

Ronan blinked, looking confused for a moment, and then sighed. "You don't have to do that."

She shook her head unable to speak for a moment, and called the office first in case Jim was already there. She stood and walked to the window, trying to steady her voice as the answering machine beeped. "Jim, I need to take a personal day. Um… I just need to do some stuff and I won't be able to make it in. Call if you need anything. Thanks." Then she texted him for good measure. *Jim, I can't come in today. Sorry to not give you any notice, but I need to deal with something. Call if you need anything.*

A moment later, Jim responded. *Are you all right?*

I don't know. I'm not sick or in the hospital or anything. Nothing you can do right now. Thanks.

He replied, *Be safe.*

She smiled a little. He really was a good boss, despite the weeks of uncharacteristic grumpiness. She sent similar texts to Heather, knowing her friend would ask Jim about her absence.

She turned to see Ronan still at the table, looking across the little living room at the pear tree and the partridge serenely staring back at him. "How are you doing?" she asked.

He blinked. "Fine." And he smiled, green-gold eyes sparkling with warmth and kindness, and something twisted inside her until she could scarcely breathe.

"What do you want to do today?" she asked, her voice shaking.

"I've never been in the museums. But perhaps you've seen them all already."

"I'd love to see them again."

They drove over the Potomac River into Washington, DC, and through the many traffic lights to park along The National Mall. Charlotte paid the meter as Ronan looked over her shoulder with interest.

Twelve Days of (Faerie) Christmas

They began at the National Museum of American History. Charlotte couldn't help smiling, despite the heaviness in her heart, when she saw that Ronan was looking around in wide-eyed excitement.

"I have to see everything!" he breathed.

He apparently meant it literally. He started at the earliest exhibit and moved slowly through the museum, examining everything in detail and reading every placard. "Did you know all this?" he murmured to her. "Is this the history you grew up with?"

"Well, I'd forgotten a lot of it. But I've been to the museums several times since I moved here." She smiled and added, "It's fun to see people excited about it."

He smiled quietly. "This is a gift, Charlotte. I lived through some of these things, but had no idea of the import at the time, nor of the direction the world would move. I was much too distracted by my own duties, and my time in this world was always quite limited."

"Have you always worked in DC?" She winced the strangeness of the question. "I mean, when you're in the human world." That sounded even stranger.

Charmed by her blush, he said with a smile, "Not always, no, but for quite some time."

They ate overpriced deli food in the food court. Ronan was delighted by each new flavor. "This is amazing." He closed his eyes in bliss while eating raspberry sorbet. They continued their tour after lunch, until Charlotte said, "There's a whole wing we haven't seen, but the museums all close at 6:00. Do you want to go over to the National Gallery of Art for the rest of the afternoon?"

He turned to her with wide eyes. "There's more?" So they walked out onto the sidewalk and turnedtoward the National Gallery of Art. "What's that one?" He pointed at the huge building between the museum they had left and their destination.

"The National Museum of Natural History. Rocks and fossils and stuff."

Ronan said nothing else, and Charlotte glanced up at him. The expression of aching loss on his face brought tears to her eyes.

Conscious of their limited time before the museum closed, Charlotte cajoled Ronan into skipping some of the exhibits to focus on the Impressionists and others she thought he would enjoy best.

"It's beautiful," he whispered when they stood in front of her favorite painting by Thomas Cole. He stepped closer to read the placard, then stepped back again, drinking in the colors and depth. "Oh, to be able to create such art!"

In an instant, she imagined giving him a gift of art classes. She imagined tubes of paint, jars of paint brushes, and stacked canvases beneath the window of her living room, near their two easels in the corner.

"Thank you for showing me this, Charlotte," he said softly, tearing his eyes away from the painting to look down at her.

"You're welcome." Her voice shook.

His lips parted, as if he wanted to say something, but then he only pressed them together and smiled. It was almost convincing.

They didn't leave until the museum closed, then they ate at an upscale grille just off the Mall.

"This feels expensive, like that place we went with Jim," Ronan murmured to her as they stepped inside. "Is that bad?" He bent to hear her answer, and his curls tickled her cheek.

"Your geese left a dragon's hoard of jewels on my hearth again this morning. I think I can buy you dinner," she whispered back.

"They're *your* geese," he said seriously. He leaned against the wall while the waiter shuffled menus.

"How's your ankle?" she asked.

"Fine." And he smiled, pale and tired and entirely at ease, and she wished—oh she wished!—for things to be different.

Dinner was exquisite. Ronan asked her about her favorite books, which exhibits she'd most enjoyed, and which paintings she loved best. His presence was easy and comforting, and the warmth in his eyes made her forget for whole minutes that their time was running short.

As they drove home, she blushed when she realized he was staring at her profile. "What is it?" she asked.

"I was just thinking…" He hesitated, then said, "Well, that today would have been immensely enjoyable with nearly any company at all, but it was much the richer for your presence."

Charlotte caught her lower lip between her teeth, trying not to weep. She heard his soft intake of breath and knew that he saw, but he said nothing, letting her compose herself in silence.

At home, they sat on the sofa in a comfortable, weary silence. The turtledoves squabbled over which one would get to sit upon Ronan's head, and the French hens huddled around his feet. Even the geese, never particularly affectionate, waddled over one by one so he could rub a finger down each of their beaks in greeting. They ruffled their feathers at him contentedly.

A pounding on the door startled them both. Ronan closed his eyes in frustration. "I'll get it," he said darkly.

He limped to the door and opened it, only to groan in frustration. "No! Go away, Garbhan! And all your brothers, too."

"Apologies, your lordship, but His Highness gave us orders." The little man pushed the door open, and Ronan glowered at him as he stumped in. Eleven others followed, crowding into Charlotte's little living room. Four had to stand on the stairs because the room was full; the geese and hens refused to give way to the serious little men.

Charlotte felt as though she could not catch her breath. "What is this?" she cried. "Who are you? And why are you here?" They looked like they were out of a movie set in Middle Earth, but smaller and a little leaner. Each wore a bright green cap.

"I'm Lord Garbhan, and these are my brothers, the lords Gofraidh, Greagoir, Geralt, Domhnall, Diarmaid, Amhlaoibh, Bairre, Carthach, Cathair, Padraig, and Oisin." The little man's dark eyes were bright with mirth.

Charlotte blinked at the onslaught of unfamiliar names, wondering if they would be offended if they knew she'd promptly forgotten them all.

"Any particular reason why you're here?" muttered Ronan.

"Orders, your lordship." His grin deepened, and she trembled at his audacity.

"But why?" she cried. "And are you magical too?"

Garbhan threw his head back and laughed.

"They're leprechauns," Ronan said. "This is one of His Majesty Cormac's elite security squads."

"But why are they here?" Charlotte frowned at him.

"Extra precautions," Lord Garbhan said seriously.

"Fine," Ronan muttered. "Make yourselves comfortable, I suppose." He waved vaguely at the living room, and Charlotte gaped at him.

"How long will they stay?"

"Oh, not long, I imagine. After midnight, I doubt there will be a need for them." Ronan sighed. "I'd hoped... well, no matter."

"Hoped what?" she asked quietly.

Lord Garbhan smiled slyly. "My brothers and I will take positions outside, Lord Ronan. We beg your pardon for the intrusion." He led the others outside, where they leapt down the stairs and stationed themselves up and down the street.

Ronan limped through the kitchen to look out the back window, then nodded.

The living room was perfectly clean and tidy, but Charlotte felt as though a whirlwind had swept through the house.

"What happens now?" she asked.

"I'd hoped..." Ronan pressed his lips together and looked down. "I'd hoped..." There was a strange, rough grief in his voice that made something twist inside Charlotte. He cleared his throat and said softly, "I'd hoped that we might have a little more time together. I wish I'd realized earlier."

"Realized what?" Charlotte could barely speak.

Ronan glanced at the clock on the microwave. "Oh, we have so little time!" He covered his mouth with one hand, his gaze flicking from the birds to the pear tree and back to the clock. "Might we go on a walk, please? Before it all goes bang?"

She stared at him. "A walk? Aren't you tired? Won't it hurt your ankle?"

"Not for long," he said softly. "I'd like to see the stars of this human world before the spell ends. See the streetlights and hear the sounds you've enjoyed for years. Feel the wind and snow on my face."

"You haven't had enough of wind and snow in the past two weeks?"

"I haven't experienced them with your hand in mine." He swallowed, and though he said nothing else, she saw the plea in his eyes.

She nodded, and they stepped outside, hand in hand.

They meandered through the neighborhood to the tiny park at the end of the street, where Ronan gallantly brushed the snow off a bench before she sat down. Snow fell softly, creating halos around the streetlights.

The colley birds murmured from a nearby tree, and small shadows formed a perimeter around the park. Moonlight glinted on the snow.

"Lift your arm," Charlotte urged, and when he did so, she scooted under it. He wrapped his arm around her, long fingers curving around her arm protectively.

She felt him sigh.

"It's a good end, I think," he said quietly. "There are things I would have done differently, if I'd been wiser and kinder. Words I would have spoken, if I were a better man. But all in all, I'm satisfied." He squeezed her gently, and she twisted to look up at him. He looked down to meet her eyes. "It's a rare gift to meet such an end in the presence of such a courageous, beautiful woman. I could ask for nothing more."

She trembled and closed her eyes, wishing she could say something, anything, to reassure him.

The slow, steady movement of his chest soothed her, and they sat in silence. She laced her fingers through his, both heedless of the cold.

Snowflakes danced in the yellow glow of the streetlights and the silver light of the moon. The cold sank into Charlotte's legs and back, and still they sat, breathing together in the winter silence.

Far in the distance a siren wailed.

Huge snowflakes landed with soft, pattering sounds. A colley bird fluttered its wings, complaining about the cold, and subsided into silence.

Church bells rang midnight.

Ronan stiffened and sucked in a breath, his eyes wide. He gave a strange, low groan of pain.

"What's wrong?" she gasped.

His breath shuddered out of him, and he stiffened. He slid off the bench and fell to his knees in the snow.

Tears slid down her cheeks unnoticed.

His face grew white, as if he were turning to stone, and his mouth opened soundlessly.

If it had to end now, there was only one thing to do.

She fell to her knees beside him and pressed her lips to his, long and hard and desperate.

He convulsed, bruising her lips against her teeth.

Then he wrapped his arms around her and kissed her in earnest, his tears dampening her cheeks as he pulled her closer.

"I thought you were dying!" she cried.

"So did I!" He flopped onto his back and laughed aloud. "Oh, my clever, tricksy, faithful friend! Cormac, I owe you my life and more."

"I know." Cormac's cool voice floated over the snow to them, and Charlotte shot to her feet, icy terror shooting through her veins.

Ronan sputtered in surprise and struggled to rise, one hand braced on the icy bench.

Cormac strolled closer, his steps measured and graceful. "Peace, Charlotte. You've nothing to fear from me." A purple bruise covered his jaw and cheek, and he spoke through swollen lips.

Ronan straightened, then deliberately knelt. "Forgive me, Cormac."

The Fae prince clasped his hand and hauled him to his feet. "Did you really think me so faithless?" he said softly. "Do you not know me better after all these years?"

"I should have," Ronan agreed. He pressed his lips together and bowed his head. "I was wrong."

"Indeed." Cormac stood silent for a moment, then gave a slight, elegant shrug. "No matter. What's done is done." He flicked his hand, and an iridescent sphere appeared in his palm. "Would you like this?"

Ronan's eyes widened. "After everything, you'd give me that?"

"What is it?" whispered Charlotte.

"It's safe passage in Faerie, on my authority, as long as I live. Even my father has no right to challenge it," Cormac said. He licked his lips, then said softly, "Do you want it?"

"You're too generous," said Ronan. "You know I do."

Cormac smiled. "We've been friends a long time, Ronan. I'd hate to have to come to the human world every time I want a good game of web-and-claw." He tossed the bubble at Ronan, who let it hit his chest. The bubble popped in a cloud of sparkles. With a flick of his wrist, he made another bubble and glanced sidelong at Charlotte. "Would you like one too?"

She swallowed fear, feeling hope rise in its place. "No strings?" she whispered.

Cormac's eyes glinted in the starlight. "Fairy gifts always have strings attached. But these strings are all for me; the gift will cost you nothing, now or ever."

At her tentative nod, he tossed her the bubble, and it popped with a similar cloud of sparkles. The feeling of warmth startled her, a sensation of fizzing energy that made each tiny hair stand on end.

Cormac hesitated, then licked his lips. "Well, then, that's done." He cleared his throat and smiled, bowed sharply, and began to walk away.

"Wait!" Ronan cried.

The Fae prince turned, pale eyebrows raised.

"Thank you, my prince."

"You're welcome." Cormac bowed slightly. "Charlotte, it has been an honor."

"The honor is mine," she whispered.

They walked back to her townhouse in a haze of relief and joy. Ronan leaned hard on his cane, and she asked, "Couldn't Cormac heal your ankle?"

He smiled. "No, Fae can't meddle in human bodies. If it were his own ankle, sure; even if I were Fae, he could probably speed the healing. But since I'm human, he can do little more than splint it, like a human doctor. He cheated a little when he set the bone, just nudged things back where they were meant to be. Like surgery but faster."

"If you're human, you should be able to take a pain-killer or something!"

He shrugged. "It's not so bad." She almost rolled her eyes, but then he smiled and said softly, "Besides, I feel like I can fly now."

He waved a graceful salute to the leprechauns and colley birds, then closed the door behind himself and leaned against it, his eyes closed. Charlotte tugged his hand gently, and he smiled, green-gold eyes searching her face.

"Sit down, then," she murmured.

He took a deep, shuddering breath, and nodded, unable to speak for a moment.

When he had composed himself and they had set-tled on the sofa, Charlotte asked, "I'm not sure I under-stand exactly what happened."

"He used the engagement spell, along with true love's first kiss, to generate enough power to break his father's hold on me." Ronan sighed. "I wonder that I did not see it, but… he concealed it so well. If it didn't work, if the attempt failed, there would be repercussions. His father would search my mind for any hint of disloyalty. I had to believe the ruse utterly in order to be entirely in-nocent.

"And, perhaps, he wanted me to feel that sense of betrayal. Perhaps my pain endeared me to you in some way; perhaps you might not have kissed me at that exact moment if you did not feel such compassion toward one you felt to be suffering unjustly."

"Well, I don't regret it."

He huffed a soft breath of mingled laughter and re-lief. "Oh, am I glad of that! I regret only that I judged him so harshly. Yet the magic looked... it looked exactly as I have said. A love spell, wrapping tighter around you with every gift! Spikes of destructive magic growing from you inch by inch, razor sharp and glittering with power. I couldn't see it until that moment in the mirror—the spikes were all pointed at me. What I thought was entrapping you was merely drawing power from your affection, the spell waiting and building with each word between us, each moment of understanding. It ticked down to the midnight on the twelfth day, to the moment of truth. Would you kiss me? And if you did, would there be enough love in it to break my imprisonment?"

The fire flickered cheerfully. Charlotte shivered, and Ronan tightened his arm around her.

"What hurt at the end? Was the spell really killing you?"

Ronan frowned faintly. "No, but... it was wrapped so tightly I could not breathe, nor could my heart beat. Perhaps it would have let go, if you hadn't kissed me. It was a side effect of the spell ripping apart my imprison-ment. I doubt Cormac did it on purpose."

Charlotte thought otherwise, but she didn't mention it. Cormac might indeed be clever enough, and manipu-lative enough, to add that little bit of drama in his at-tempt to ensure Charlotte kissed Ronan. Yet she couldn't decide if he was wrong to do so. What if she hadn't kissed him?

"I have nothing to offer, Charlotte." His eyes searched her face. "Nothing but love, I mean. Strong enough for the spell to use, yet not nearly as strong as it will grow, increasing as it does moment by moment with you."

She almost blushed in the warmth of his gaze, almost looked away from the bright hope shining in his eyes. Instead, she said, "I thought it was *my* love that broke the spell."

For an instant he stopped breathing, and then he laughed, deep and joyous. He pressed a kiss to her cheek and murmured in her ear, "Let me prove it was mine, Charlotte. I'll show you how it grows year by year, and I'll count every moment a gift."

ABOUT THE AUTHOR

C. J. Brightley lives in Northern Virginia with her husband and young children. She holds degrees from Clemson University and Texas A&M. She welcomes visitors and messages at her website, www.cjbrightley.com.

THINGS UNSEEN

A LONG-FORGOTTEN SONG
BOOK 1

CHAPTER 1

Researching this thesis is an exercise in dedication, frustration, making up stuff, pretending I know what I'm doing, and wondering why nothing adds up. Aria swirled her coffee and stared at the blank page in her notebook.

Why did I decide to study history? She flipped back to look at her notes and sighed. She couldn't find enough information to even form a coherent thesis. The records were either gone, or had never existed in the first place. *Something* had happened when the Revolution came to power, but she didn't know what, and she couldn't even pinpoint exactly when.

The nebulous idea she'd had for her research seemed even more useless now. She'd been trying to find records of how things had changed since the Revolution, how the city had grown and developed. There were official statistics on the greater prosperity, the academic success of the city schools, and the vast reduction in crime. The statistics didn't mention the abandoned buildings, the missing persons, or any grumbling against the curfew. At least it was later now; for a year, curfew had been at dusk.

She glanced around the bookstore at the other patrons. A man wearing a business suit was browsing in the self-help section, probably trying to improve his public speaking. A girl, probably another student judging by her worn jeans and backpack, was sitting on the floor in the literary fiction section, completely engrossed in a book.

Aria flipped to the front of the book again. It was a memoir of someone she'd never heard of. She'd picked it up almost at random, and flipped to the middle, hoping to find something more interesting than dead ends. The words told of a walk in the forest, and for a moment Aria was there, her nose filled with the scents of pine and loam, her eyes dazzled by the sunlight streaming through the leaves swaying above her. She blinked, and the words were there but the feeling was gone. Rereading the passage, she couldn't figure out why she'd been caught up with such breathless realism.

It wasn't that the words were so profound; she was confident they were not. Something had caught her though, and she closed her eyes to imagine the forest again, as if it were a memory. Distant, faded, perhaps not even her memory. A memory of something she'd seen in a movie, perhaps, or a memory of a dream she'd had as a child.

Something about it troubled her, and she meant to come back to it. Tonight, though, she had other homework, and she pushed the book aside.

Dandra's Books was an unassuming name for the

best bookstore in all of the North Quadrant. Dandra was a petite, grey-haired lady with a warm smile. She also had the best map collection, everything from ancient history, both originals and reproductions, to modern maps of cities both near and far, topographical maps, water currents, and everything else. She carried the new releases and electronic holdings that were most in demand, but what made the store unique was the extensive and ever-changing selection of used and antique books. If it could be found, Dandra could find it. Aria suspected she maintained an unassuming storefront because she didn't want demand to increase; business was sufficient to pay the bills and she refused to hire help.

Dandra also made tolerable coffee, an important consideration for a graduate student. Aria had spent hours studying there as an undergraduate; it had the same air of productive intellectualism as the university library, but without the distraction of other groups of students having more fun than she was. She'd found it on a long, meandering walk avoiding some homework. Something about the place made concentrating easier.

Except when it came to her thesis. Aria told herself that she was investigating what resources were available before she narrowed her focus. But sometimes, when she stared at the blank pages, she almost admitted to herself the truth, that she was frustrated with her professors, her thesis, and the Empire itself. She didn't have a good explanation, and she hadn't told anyone.

Something about this image of the forest felt true in a way that nothing had felt for a very long time. It was evidence. Evidence of *what*, she wasn't sure. But definitely evidence.

She finished her homework and packed her bag. She put a bookmark in the memoir and reshelved it, resolving that she would come back later and read it a bit more. It was already late, and she had an early class the next day.

After class there were errands, and homework, and more class, and lunch with a boy who'd seemed almost likable until he talked too much about his dysfunctional family and his abiding love for his ex-girlfriend, who lived down the hall in his apartment building. It was a week before she made it back to Dandra's.

The book was gone.

Dandra shook her head when Aria asked about it. "I don't know what book you mean. I've never had a book like that."

Aria stared at her in disbelief. "You saw me read it last week. It was called *Memories Kept* or something like that. *Memory Keeper*, maybe. Don't you remember? I was sitting there." She pointed.

Dandra gave her a sympathetic look. "You've been studying too much, Aria. I'm sorry. I don't have that book. I don't think I ever did."

Aria huffed in frustration and bought a cup of coffee. She put too much sugar and cream in it and sat by the window at the front. She stared at the people as they came in, wondering if her anger would burn a hole in the back of someone's coat. It didn't, but the mental picture amused her.

Not much else did. The thesis was going nowhere, and the only thing that kept her interest was a line of questions that had no answers and a book that didn't exist.

Was the degree worth anything anyway? She'd studied history because she enjoyed stories, wanted to learn about the past. But the classes had consisted almost entirely of monologues by the professors about the strength of the Empire and how much better things were now after the Revolution. Her papers had alternated between parroting the professors' words, and uneasy forays into the old times. The research was hard, and getting harder.

The paper she'd written on the Revolution, on how John Sanderhill had united the warring factions, had earned an F. Dr. Corten had written "Your implication that Sanderhill ordered the assassination of Gerard Neeson is patently false and betrays an utter lack of understanding of the morality of the Revolution. I am unable to grade this paper higher than an F, in light of such suspect scholarship and patriotism." Yet Aria had cited her source clearly and had been careful not to take a side on the issue, choosing merely to note that it was one possible explanation for Neeson's disappearance at the height of the conflict. Not even the most likely.

For a history department, her professors were remarkably uninterested in exploring the past. She scowled at her coffee as it got colder. What was the point of history, if you couldn't learn from it? The people in history weren't perfect, any more than people now were. But surely, as scholars, they should be able to admit that imperfect people and imperfect decisions could yield lessons and wisdom.

It wasn't as if it was ancient history either. The Revolution had begun less than fifteen years ago. One would think information would be available. Memories should be clear.

But they weren't.

The man entered Dandra's near dusk. He wore no jacket against the winter cold, only a threadbare short-sleeved black shirt. His trousers were dark and equally worn, the cuffs skimming bare ankles. His feet were bare too, and that caught her attention.

He spoke in a low voice, but she was curious, so she listened hard and heard most of what he said. "I need the maps, Dandra."

"You know I don't have those."

"I'll pay."

"I don't have them." Dandra took a step back as he leaned forward with his hands resting on the desk. "I told you before, I can't get them. I still can't."

"I was told you could on good authority." His voice stayed very quiet, but even Aria could hear the cold anger. "Should I tell Petro he was wrong about you?"

"Are you threatening me?" Dandra's eyes widened, but Aria couldn't tell if it was in fear or in anger.

"I'm asking if Petro was wrong."

"Tell Petro I did my best. I couldn't get them." Dandra clasped her hands together and drew back, her shoulders against the wall, and Aria realized she was terrified. Of the man in the black shirt, or of Petro, or possibly both.

Aria rose. "Excuse me? Can I help you find something?" She smiled brightly at him.

He stared at Dandra for a long moment, then turned away. He brushed past Aria and out the door without looking at her, and disappeared into the darkness.

Dandra looked at her with wide eyes. "That wasn't wise, but thank you."

"Who is he?"

Dandra shook her head. "Don't ask questions you don't want to know the answer to. Go home, child. It's late."

Made in the USA
Middletown, DE
16 December 2018